COURTING THE COUNTESS

When Melissa Neville, widowed Countess of Pateley, suffers life-threatening injuries in a fire, no one expects her to survive long. However, despite her disfigurement, would-be suitors have been a constant intrusion, all of them hoping to get their hands on her fortune before she expires. Then one night, in the privacy of her bath, she is abducted without explanation by Colonel Harry Gunn and his steward Zed, who specialise in medicine and seem to want to help her. What is their real motive — and can Melissa hope to love again?

ANNE STENHOUSE

COURTING THE COUNTESS

Complete and Unabridged

LINFORD
Leicester

First published in Great Britain in 2016

First Linford Edition
published 2019

A catalogue record for this book is available
from the British Library.

ISBN 978–1–4448–4008–7

Published by
F. A. Thorpe (Publishing)
Anstey, Leicestershire

Set by Words & Graphics Ltd.
Anstey, Leicestershire
Printed and bound in Great Britain by
T. J. International Ltd., Padstow, Cornwall

This book is printed on acid-free paper

Dedication: For the members, Past and Present, of Edinburgh Writers' Club. Their support over the years has been warmly appreciated.

1

Borders, Northumberland, 1819

Melissa stood as still as her injuries allowed. Soapy water drained down her skin into the tin bath, making her shiver in the night air. A tiny breeze riffled through the steam and made her wonder if the bedroom door had opened.

'Allow me, ma'am. Your maid is unable to come to your assistance.'

The calm words slammed shock through Melissa. How had a stranger gained entry? Where was Joanie? And Simmerton? Percy? Even young Matt? Why had no one raised an alarm?

'A word from you to ensure your maid's good behaviour would release her from Zed's hold. She is struggling so hard she may injure herself.' Because he still spoke without heat or temper or lust, Melissa thought he was used to command.

'Allow me, please.' The man and his mellow voice came nearer. Scottish? She furrowed her brow. Why would a Scot be here? Warm breath fanned her neck as he leant in towards her. It was already too late to do anything in her own defence.

Melissa had not expected to meet any man in her bedroom. Men, in her reduced health, were so much more challenging than when she had been in her prime. Then, she'd laughed off the attentions of enough treasure-hunting suitors to fill the ranks of a regiment. She'd sent even the obnoxious lawyer Withershaws off with a clear understanding that neither his advice nor his person were wanted by her.

She shuddered. Best not to allow memories of that interview to disturb her reasoning when she needed to stay calm.

It's so uncivilised to be found like this. No covering for my scars and without my wig. Naked. Vulnerable. Furious. Puzzled. Why doesn't he recoil?

She resisted the temptation to spread her fingers over the tightly curling stubble that was growing through her scalp. She choked back a scream. She tamped down the idea she might escape. Whatever else she'd learned in the aftermath of the fire, the knowledge there was no escape was first and foremost on her list. She would face this voyeur as she had faced all the others.

Towels swathed her shoulders gently, although the scarring down her right side did not react. Large hands offered her support and took her weight with ease as she stepped from the bath onto more thick towelling.

It's as if he's handing me down from a carriage and holding my parasol while I adjust my skirts.

She turned her head to see a large male in riding clothes. He was dressed like a gentleman, but what did that

3

mean in the new world Melissa inhabited? She gripped the towelling close and suddenly felt tingling in her damaged right arm.

'My arm . . . '

'Have I hurt you, ma'am?'

'No, but I feel sensations I did not have earlier. Perhaps the shocking nature of your intrusion has pumped blood through my damaged veins.' She focussed on his face with its pronounced cheekbones. They gave it interesting shape.

The man sought her eyes and kept his gaze fixed. Every physician who'd seen what this stranger had now seen had blenched. Her maid found it an effort to spread salve night and morning despite seeing the scars daily.

'You do not back away, sir,' Melissa challenged the intruder. 'Perhaps your way of life inures you to such horror?' His appearance was familiar, but she was sure she hadn't met him before. How could any woman forget such god-like beauty? His hair was a

4

sun-kissed blond mop and set off features of perfect symmetry. She thought no sculptor could ever do better. In candlelight, it was a fleeting impression, but Melissa felt this man was special.

She sent her gaze around the room and saw Simmerton just outside in the corridor. The butler's hands were tied before him and he leant, eyes closed, against the wall.

'You've beaten Simmerton,' she exclaimed. 'What kind of coward attacks an old man? Look at your handiwork.' Fury rose within her as she took in the butler's injuries. Why had he not called out? Why had she sent the younger footmen away?

Because he and Joanie are the only people left in this world I can trust — and now I've put them in danger, too. Where is Joanie? Why would she injure herself?

A bruise was darkening Simmerton's skin below an eye. She saw the intruder flush as the truth of her words hit home. She hoped his embarrassment was a good sign but wondered how long the household staff below stairs would be unaware of events in the house. They were her only hope of rescue, because now Joanie was brought into the room dangling from the arm of another male, a rougher individual whose dark-eyed stare was nonetheless full of compassion — or pity. The girl was held around her waist and she kicked and struggled, fiercely berating her captor in colourful language.

'Stop it, girl,' the rough man said, 'or your hands will be next to be tied and then your feet.' Joanie threw the basin of salve she carried at the young god, and brought her elbow back to wind her attacker. 'Enough!' the man yelled, dropping her to the floor and stooping to bring her slender arm up behind her back.

The younger man lifted a hand and scooped salve from his clothes where the bowl had discharged its precious contents. He held the hand away and wrinkled his nose.

'Is it comfrey?' He seemed inordinately pleased when he thought he'd identified the main ingredient in her salve, but then he realised a melée was developing. 'Let her go,' he snapped. 'Ma'am,' he said, turning back to Melissa, 'Colonel Harry Gunn, at your service.' He bowed.

Melissa knew then why he was familiar. 'He has sent you to murder me.'

'No one will murder you.'

Joanie moved as quickly as a ferret released from a sack and grabbed the window pole from its position behind the curtains. In seconds, the rough man snatched it from her and tossed it aside like so much kindling. He unravelled a length of twine from his waist and was beginning to wrap it around the girl's wrists when Gunn spoke again.

'Leave her be, Zed; and you, girl, settle down. We mean none of you harm, and must move as quickly as we can to be out of here before the laundry workers return to the yards.'

'Surely a parcel of drunken laundry maids will surely be nothing to brave men like you. After all, sir, you've subdued an unarmed retainer and a serving maid.' Melissa threw the words at his head and saw the quick blush darken his features again. *Who is Colonel Gunn*, she wondered, *if not George Gunn's brother?*

'I trust my behaviour from now on will refute your accusations, Lady Pateley, but there is no time to explain it.' He drew his clean hand through his hair, and Melissa watched the thick locks fall back into disorder. The sort of disorder young men paid their valets to study and achieve for them, she thought; or did military men simply favour disorder?

'Time is something I have in plenty, Colonel. I no longer do the social round.'

'No, ma'am — you don't have any time to spare, please believe me. Your maid will assist you to dress. I regret

her basin is now empty,' he said, and
cast a rueful glance down the front of
his caped riding coat. 'So if the salve
was a nightly application, it must be
missed today. Although,' he added,
looking into his right hand, 'there is a
dollop here.'

Before Melissa could see what he was
about, the colonel pressed her onto a
stool and reached down to flick back
her towels. His hand moved calmly over
the worst of the burns, which lay across
the shoulder blade on her right side.
She started, but he kept her seated by
placing his other hand on her left
shoulder, and continued to stroke the
salve he'd scraped from his coat into
her weeping flesh. His hand was gentle
and rhythmic.

When she dared to look up, she saw
Zed had left her bedroom with
Simmerton, and Joanie was standing,
open-mouthed, in shock. A chemise
dangled from the girl's hands and her
hair was tumbling around her white
features.

'There,' Colonel Gunn said, 'I hope it will serve. But if you have further supplies in the abbey we should collect them to take with us. It may be some days before an apothecary can be found.'

Melissa drew her towel around her again and looked up at the big man. His complexion might be pinker than it had been, she thought. 'You are little discomfited by ministering to a naked and scarred countess you've never met before,' she challenged him.

'I treat my own horses, you must know. Always have done.'

'I wonder whether I am relieved to learn you view me as one of your injured fillies, Colonel. Please leave me now.' Anger fired her. Certainly, it was no fault of Gunn's she'd been trapped in a fire by falling timber, but his words reminded her of how far she'd come along the road into obscurity. She wondered if the mists of social myth already surrounding her name were what allowed Gunn to compare her to

10

his horses. She was a suffering beast in his eyes; no more but not less.

Henry Gunn bowed and stepped towards the door, but he stopped and turned back. Melissa could not mistake the tension in his muscles that drew him to his full impressive height. In that moment she knew he was a dangerous man.

'Lady Pateley, we will leave here as soon as you are clothed, and sooner if my men have not succeeded in delaying the laundry-wife and her maids. Do not think I will hesitate to wrap you naked in the carriage rugs.' He left then, and Melissa stared at the space he'd vacated.

Wrap me in rugs, will you, sir! I think not.

'The back entrance, Joanie,' she hissed to the girl as they struggled to get her into some clothing. 'It takes a spiral stair down into the old library, which has doors to the terrace. We can slide along the wall of the house and reach the gate into the walled garden.'

Melissa pulled on her boots. Pain screamed through the damaged muscles of her right arm, but she gritted her teeth and carried on. How could she even think of leaving her sanctuary in the company of George Gunn's brother? The fire may have been a fortuitous accident for the man, she knew, but his persistent attempts to capture her since were sinister.

'You're right, my lady, the path goes down to the drying greens,' Joanie whispered back. 'We should meet the laundry staff or find one of the gardeners.' Melissa watched the girl grab the window pole again and thrust it through the wooden bars on both bedroom doors. Hadn't she installed them for this kind of eventuality? A makeshift barrier at best.

Working together, they drew the cupboard that concealed the staircase door away from it. Joanie turned the huge key and held a lighted candle high. Melissa was wrung out with the pain of shifting such a huge obstacle, and she felt Joanie's concerned gaze raking her features.

'Let me, your ladyship, please,' the girl said. Reluctantly, Melissa leaned on her arm and began the descent.

Fresh night air wafted into the dank stairwell and brought the smell of her salve. When she raised her head, Gunn's stained coat confronted her.

'You would have found it much easier to leave by the normal route,' the colonel said. 'However, we have brought a carriage round.'

With no further words, he stooped and lifted Melissa over one shoulder. She heard a scuffle and knew the rougher man, Zed, had taken Joanie up in the same manner. They were handed up to other men inside the carriage, and once Gunn and Zed replaced those helpers, it jolted into motion.

Melissa heard the wheels of another coach scrunch across gravel and hoped Simmerton had been left to raise the alarm. Was Simmerton still alive? The thought brought her eyes wide open, and she glared at the colonel.

'My staff?'

'Your people are unharmed beyond Simmerton's black eye. He is in the following coach. We set him and a footman to collect some of your belongings and have to hope mere men will have made a goodish selection.' He straightened his legs, and Melissa tucked hers closer to her side of the vehicle. 'There was a stone jar of the salve which the butler pointed out.'

Melissa's head swam with exhaustion and she felt her eyes close. The cushion beside her sprang as Joanie was pulled across the coach to make way for Gunn to sit beside her. He gathered her into a blanket and lifted her across his lap with her injured side uppermost.

'Sleep, Lady Pateley. We have many miles to travel.'

∗ ∗ ∗

The carriage drew to a standstill and slowly Melissa came awake. She stirred

14

in the arms of a man for the first time in years, three years in fact. Three years of being a widow.

'You are awake, ma'am,' Colonel Gunn said, and Melissa focussed her uninjured left eye on the stubble that shadowed his strong chin and delineated the bones of his jaw-line. Attractive as the sight was, she didn't need to spend time wondering why such a virile man had chosen to abduct her. If he wasn't acting on behalf of George Gunn, then perhaps he was just like all the others. Melissa, Countess of Pateley was the richest widow in the kingdom, and everyone expected she would succumb to her injuries sooner rather than later.

Melissa drew a deep breath. It was disappointing to be courted by so many men who assured her of her increasing health while they counted on her early demise. Many wished to be her consort in order to be left in charge of her fortune. Very few had any inclination to be saddled with a woman whose reputation included not only renowned intellect, but persistent pursuit of her own way in life.

'I am awake, sir. Where are we?' She could hear wind soughing among trees and the restless shuffling of many horses. 'Did you bring a platoon to kidnap me?'

She felt Gunn's strong thigh muscles contract beneath her, and she groaned when he thrust her off his lap into a sitting position. *I've annoyed him*, she thought with satisfaction.

'I do wish you would keep your conclusions about my behaviour and intentions to yourself until they are better informed,' he said testily.

'I was bathing in my own property, and you forcibly removed me with my butler and maid . . . '

'And two footmen. Percy, I think, and Matt.'

Melissa's heart gave a tiny leap of satisfaction to hear that. She knew how much of her survival over the last two months she owed to this close-knit little band of staff. 'Are the men injured?'

'No, your ladyship. The men showed remarkable common sense, and being invited at pistol point to collect your boxes worked speedily.' Melissa glanced at the other man now because he spoke. Zed — was that what the colonel had called him?

'I see, Mr Zed.'

'Just Zed,' he muttered, and Melissa had to hold her gaze steady before his censorious one. What was the matter with these men, that they believed she should be grateful for being abducted?

'We'll make camp overnight,' Gunn said, breaking into the increasingly aggressive exchange. 'The moon has gone and it's too dangerous to continue. We might lose a horse or tip a carriage into a rut.'

'Make camp,' Melissa said in disbelief. 'I am not one of your soldiers, sir.'

Across the confined space, Zed grunted and then rose. The carriage shook as his weight upset the balance. Joanie squealed and clung to a strap.

Melissa looked at the girl, and even in the near dark could see how afraid she was. They were alone in a forest, she supposed, with a platoon of soldiers. How disciplined were they? Melissa wondered. They had no doubt been discharged after the tyrant Napoleon was sent to St Helena. Many were reduced to all sorts to make any kind of living, and many would have no decent homes behind them to exert good influence.

Melissa had no fears for herself. She was scarred and crippled by the fire. Most people found it hard to look at her. Joanie, however, was young and attractive. Melissa was nervous on her behalf. It would not be good to aggravate their captors.

'Well, it will be something of an adventure for us, won't it, Joanie?' She injected as much colour into her voice as she could without making it too false. Joanie was young, but she was not a child.

'If you say so, my lady. I prefers my

bed to the beasties and all we'll get on the bare ground.' Melissa privately agreed with this depressing observation, but did not say so.

Zed grunted again, but as he'd dismounted by now, they were not treated to another glare.

'Lady Pateley, the men will cut branches and lay some thin mattresses over them for you and the girl. There are tents and blankets,' Gunn said quietly.

'Lady Pateley, my lady,' Simmerton half-shouted as he ran up from the second carriage. 'Are you quite well, my lady?'

'I am well, Simmerton. I slept most of the journey, and now I understand we are to make camp.' Melissa knew this would not please her elderly retainer, and she was hardly surprised when he protested.

'Camp? Make camp? My lady, what can you mean?'

'Tents, Simmerton. And you know, it may not rain even if we have arrived in

Scotland.' Melissa uttered the words without much thought and then wondered if her abductor would take umbrage, but she heard a quiet chuckle. She turned to study Gunn. 'I am assuming you have brought me north?'

'I have, ma'am. Can you not smell the air?' He spoke with the simple satisfaction of a native coming home.

Melissa laughed in her turn. 'How can the air smell different over a distance covered in what, two hours?'

★ ★ ★

The following day, Harry Gunn stooped to remove the spurs from his riding boots. The last part of the journey was best performed in silence. Silence and stealth had proved well matched bedfellows for the last several weeks, but he would be glad to be rid of them. Rid and purged of their necessity. A gentleman's calling held more dark necessities than Harry had dreamed of before the fire that destroyed Lady Pateley's beauty and gave George the prompt he needed.

The memory of the countess's scarring stilled his hand, and he heard again her accusation.

Surely a parcel of drunken laundry maids will be nothing to brave men like you? After all, sir, you've subdued an unarmed retainer and a serving maid. But the voice echoing in his head was his sister's. It resounded down the years, accusing him, always accusing him; and yet, he'd rarely been found to be at fault. It was as if the voice of an angry woman stilled his brain and prevented him explaining or defending himself.

He dropped the spurs into a travel bag and stood for a moment with head cocked. *I must look like one of my spaniels*, he thought, and a smile tugged at his lips. Thistle would be whelping about now, and her daughter Downie next week. How many pups? How many would he keep? When would living ever revert to the simple matters that made up the life of a Scottish laird?

He heard the signal. Two sharp whistles borne on the breeze caressed his ear. He reached up and grabbed his reins, whispering to the skittish gelding as it tugged and backed. Uncertainty gave way to pulsing need as the signal came again. It told him Zed had the Keep of Duns in his sights and all was well. Harry mounted his horse and paced along the service lane, skirting the grounds of the great house until it gave out at a complex of buildings.

'Here, Colonel,' Zed hissed from deep shadow. Harry heard Zed's horse snuffle a welcome to his own. He pulled back on the reins and dismounted. 'This is the stables, right enough.'

'Good man. Anything to suggest all is not as it should be?' Harry gazed around at his friend Colonel Thomas Paxton's well-kept grounds, and a flight of wood pigeons lifted into the air. Perhaps there would be game shooting.

'It all looks as right and tight as may be, sir. Her ladyship will be well protected here. Does Mistress Duart arrive tonight?' Zed walked his horse forward until he could peer round the entrance pend and into the square of elegant stables and carriage houses. They were quiet now, with only one or two beasts in residence, but the arrival of Harry's full complement of men and the two carriages would change all that.

'Lizzie is waiting my order at an inn in Lauder. She should be with us before the sun goes down.' Harry stopped and listened to . . .

Nothing. We are alone, with maybe a stable-hand left behind by Thomas and Agnes. Nothing feels good. What will Lady Pateley think of this?

He ran a hand around his neck beneath the loosened cloth he'd tied quickly this morning. The overnight stay in deep forest had reduced Simmerton to apoplexy, but Lady Pateley had calmed the man as if he were her aged parent and not a retainer.

'Tents, Simmerton. And you know, it may not rain even if we have arrived in

Scotland,' she'd said when it became clear there were tents and campfires, but no roofs or beds beyond cut branches woven roughly into matting.

'It may not rain.'

Harry chuckled quietly. The lady was resourceful and must have been so very beautiful before the fire. Now, eight weeks on, she was healing on the outside. How, he wondered, was she healing in her thoughts and mind? The woman would need nerves of tempered steel to withstand the onslaught of so much.

'Whae's that?' an aggressive roar went up from the stable-yard, and Harry and Zed moved forward as one. Zed raised a hand and called back to the man.

'Colonel Harry Gunn and his company. You can put your weapon down.'

The man seemed little inclined to do so, and Harry knew a moment of despair. Could they have come so far to be shot by a terrified stable-hand? Another darker thought flicked across his mind. Was the man not in fact one of Thomas's men, but one of George's?

'Did Colonel Paxton tell you the pheasants were golden in dawn light?' Harry asked, and cheered up as he saw Zed's shoulders square. He'd forgotten to offer the password question they'd long ago agreed with Thomas.

'That he did, sir. An' at dusk the feathers a' fa' out.' The groom bellowed his reply, and laughed immoderately to cover the momentary rejection of his employer's friend and guest. 'Come by and rest the horses. That's a fine head on yon lad.'

'He's called Gorse,' Harry said, glad to be able to hand his precious gelding over to someone who knew about horses. 'There are carriages which will take my passengers to the kitchen yard, and once the boxes are off they'll be round with men and twenty or so horses.'

'Then there's another carriage and several escorts awaiting the signal to come frae Lauder,' Zed said, keeping his eyes on the groom. 'Do you have a body to spare who knows the roads? Our men can take care of their own horses, and they have a cook.'

'Aye, aye.' The groom's eyes were wide in wonder, but he was well trained and didn't seek any answers yet. 'There's three here besides masel' and the colonel, Colonel Paxton that is, left fower riding horses behind. Is it a letter tae gae up to Lauder?'

Harry left Zed composing a letter for his sister's steward and walked briskly through the grounds to the back of Thomas's great house. The medieval keep from which it took its name glowered in a mass of ivy and sang with the noise of birds. It probably provided roosts for hundreds later in the day. More attractive were the additional wings Thomas's father and grandfather had added to the building. Borders stone rose over four stories, and Harry knew from earlier, happier visits, that it provided comfortable modern accommodation. Lodgings fit not only for a countess, but for his exacting sister, Lottie Duart.

The first of the carriages rolled off the drive and pulled into the kitchen courtyard as he reached the corner of the big wall that enclosed the vegetable garden. Thomas would have left staff there, too, he knew. It was August, and much would need harvesting.

★   ★   ★

Melissa gazed out onto an enclosed courtyard. *He's had them bring me to the servants' entrance*, she thought, and bristled. Colonel Gunn clearly did not want to attract attention to carriages arriving on the carriage drive, whether he was in George Gunn's pocket or acting for someone else.

The door of her vehicle was thrown open, and her young footman Percy lowered the step. The poor man could hardly bring his gaze to meet her own, but he grasped her left hand and helped her onto the flags.

'Are you steady, Lady Pateley?'

'Thank you, Percy, I am. Please assist Mr Simmerton. He was still shaky from the blow to his head when we stopped earlier.' Melissa looked across to the following carriage. How could anyone have attacked such a fragile servant? she wondered again. It did not sit well with Gunn's protestations about acting for her welfare.

'I'll do that, your ladyship,' Percy said, interrupting her thoughts. 'He were a right silly.'

'Oh?'

'To turn round that quick when Mr Zed told him to be still. He cracked his face hard against the outer doors. He told me all about it. I think he feels he let you down, your ladyship.' Percy turned away to see to the butler, and when Melissa raised her head she found the colonel was studying her.

His quiet observation was as unsettling as his attentions to her shoulder had been last night, and she felt colour threaten to flush the uninjured left side of her face. Why was he so still? It made her feel as if he regarded her like some kind of wounded animal.

Isn't that exactly what you are?

'It seems I misunderstood some of your actions last night, Colonel Gunn. I beg pardon,' she said crisply.

'Well, I don't know why you think that, ma'am, but it's gracious of you to accept your blame. Welcome to the Keep of Duns. It belongs to my friend Colonel Thomas Paxton, but he's away from home.' Gunn stepped towards her and offered his right arm, which Melissa took after a momentary hesitation. 'We are expected, but Thomas and Agnes have left only a very small staff as they've taken their people up to Edinburgh. It will take my men an hour or so to make us comfortable. I hope my sister, Mrs Duart, will have joined us by then; and if not, in time for dinner.'

'Your sister, Colonel?'

'I must have a care for your reputation, ma'am, and my sister is in need of a little diversion. Her husband is a plant collector, and at the present time he's travelling in Siam.' Gunn stood to one side while Melissa eased through the door into a back passage lined with boots and empty baskets. The air smelled strongly of fish. 'So it made perfect sense for her to join us.'

'Perfect,' Melissa agreed. 'It's such a pity she wasn't available to join us under canvas.'

'As to that, I feel should anyone ever ask, then it would be a better plan to claim we left your country seat on *this* morning and travelled in light vehicles at a spanking pace.' He slapped his hand loudly across his thigh. Melissa jumped and she heard Joanie, who was moving quietly along behind them, let out a small squeal.

'With the luggage following on,' Melissa agreed. The man was incorrigible. 'What thought did you give to my reputation when you required me to sleep out under the stars, sir?'

'I had no choice, ma'am.' Gunn

sighed. 'Although I missed the fresh air and night sounds when I first came back from the wars, I now find I miss the comfort of my bed.'

'Indeed. Perhaps your advancing years are to blame for that,' Melissa said waspishly. Privately, she had enjoyed the quiet night broken by the snuffling of their horses and the occasional shriek of a night animal. There had been no nightmare last night, and although the sleep she enjoyed had been short, it had been deep and peaceful.

'Perhaps,' Gunn agreed with her. 'On the other hand, at least last night I was awake while you slept. I may not have had a care for your reputation, but I was very careful of your person.'

Melissa was not able to study his expression in the dark back reaches of this strange house, but she thought he sounded genuine. Who was he, and what was his connection with the blackguard George? she wondered for the fiftieth time since he'd abducted her.

'Why have you abducted me?'

'And what is my connection with George Gunn — ?' The colonel moved forward, urging Melissa into the light of a grand entrance hall. 'Let us take seats in Thomas and Agnes's saloon, and I will answer some of your queries.'

2

Melissa gazed around the first-floor room with its windows in two walls. Comfortable-looking sofas sat on either side of a large fireplace, and there were deep armchairs covered in flowery chintz elsewhere in the room. Plenty of small tables and candelabra showed careful regard for the users' comfort.

At her side, the colonel sighed. She looked at him quizzically. 'It always brings me a sense of peace coming into this room, and I find it a strange experience, as Thomas was the untidiest soldier I ever shared a mess with.' He extended a hand towards the sofas and Melissa sat down. Joanie crept around the edges of the room, studying the ornaments and small paintings before she chose a seat inside the door and perched on the edge.

Joanie looks as if she's hoping for a

chance to escape. But where would we run to? My carriages have all been left behind at the abbey. Surely the staff will have sent off to Aunt Flaxxe by now? What will she do?

'You are thoughtful, ma'am,' the colonel interrupted her thoughts. 'And I know why you might be so.'

'Do you undertake to tell me how I think, Colonel Gunn? You must know many have tried before now.' Melissa bridled. Mr David Withershaws was among those many, and thoughts of him caused her eyes to flash inwardly as if she were experiencing a seizure of nervous agitation. Mr Withershaws, with his overly ingratiating manners that turned without warning into sneering disdain for anyone born female, was not here. Melissa felt limp and frail. It was madness to compare Harry Gunn, whose open face and hazel eyes were without guile of any kind she could see, with that villain.

Nonetheless, the colonel was exasperating. Why was the man so understanding of her moods? Even the few hours she'd shared with him had shown him to be intuitive beyond her experience of males. His brow furrowed. Melissa watched the rise and fall of his broad shoulders beneath the fine tweed of a tailored coat as he took a sustaining breath.

I'm working against myself by antagonising him. I would do better to simper a little, as he must be used to from the women he meets at regimental balls, and perhaps find answers that way.

'Of course, not many have the experience of a senior officer and leader of men.'

She watched in some interest as Colonel Gunn's eyebrows lifted towards the blond locks tumbling onto his forehead. Perhaps she hadn't got the intonation quite right, she thought. Simpering wasn't something she was much practised in.

'Lady Pateley, I am truly sorry to have removed you from your refuge in Berwick Old Abbey, but I was unable to guarantee your safety there,' the colonel said, and Melissa felt her own eyebrows rise.

'This is the first conundrum, Colonel. Why do you believe you owe my safety any attention whatsoever?' she snapped. Too late, she realised it wasn't at all in a simpering mode, or even perhaps civil.

'I do agree we'll deal better together if you feel able to speak honestly, ma'am.' He sat down at last, crossing the worn Turkish rug that graced the floor. His bulk swamped the sofa cushions. Those long legs she'd had to avoid last night in the carriage stretched comfortably over the floor, and she caught sight of a tuft of grass clinging to his left boot. It must have missed the scraper, she thought inconsequentially.

'So let me speak. Why . . . '

The colonel held up a palm. His smile was amused enough to make Melissa stretch a hand out, looking for something to throw at his head.

'George Gunn is my cousin. Not

particularly close . . . '

'But you look alike, sir. True you are blond where he is dark, but otherwise . . . '

'Yes, we do, and I observe in my own family and others that resemblances can be very strong when there are distances such as second cousinship. George is a descendant of my great-great-grandfather, and not very close in either blood or society.' The colonel closed down his expression, and Melissa could judge nothing of his thoughts. What, she wondered, did the Gunn family think of their cousins?

'I cannot tell what you mean by such a remark, sir. Surely all families work together to secure the good of the whole?' She kept her eyes fixed on his face, although her right one was troubling her more than a little. It still filled with tears and watered copiously at unpredictable moments. She saw Colonel Gunn watch a trickle of tears as they dripped down her cheek and onto her front.

I will not acknowledge it. He must treat me as an equal and not as an injured female in need of his protection.

'Not all family members earn such a right,' he said quietly. With a graceful thrust, he stood and came over to her. She saw the square of clean linen in his hand and shrank back against the cushions. 'Please, allow me.'

'I am more than capable of wiping away my tears, Colonel,' Melissa protested, and brought her left hand up between them to snatch the handkerchief.

'Of course.' He leant back and kept it out of her reach. 'But when you have the opportunity of being ministered to by an expert, why not allow it?' The man smiled and Melissa drew a startled breath. He was so beautiful to look at, and so different from George, whose perfect features never showed emotion of any kind.

'Colonel, this is really most unorthodox,' she protested; but even to her own ears the words were feeble and feebly uttered. His hands were again gentle and sure. There was little hair left on the right side of her head, but he pushed aside her wig and ran long fingers through the re-growth. She tensed. He lifted his concerned gaze to her face as if to check he did no harm by his exploration.

'I can see your maid has done an exceptional job, Lady Pateley. I was under the command of the Earl of Hopetoun in eight and nine during the war in the peninsula. There was much opportunity to study the treatment of injuries after the various engagements.' He sat back on his haunches and made a close study of the scarring down the side of her neck and would, Melissa felt sure, have pushed aside her clothing had she been a male. She caught his gaze and saw how right she was in thinking that. Heat flared between them, and she spoke quickly to douse it.

'The major damage was exacted on

my shoulder, which you saw last night.' She unbent a little, because he had the air of a good physician, and Melissa had now seen several of those. 'I lost much of my hair and have worn a wig since the skin on my neck healed.'

'I trust the scalp was not burned?' he asked abruptly.

'It was not, no. Simmerton threw a hessian apron over it, and the falling roof timber that trapped my upper body fizzled out quickly. However, it was alight long enough to set my clothing alight, too. That is where the burns come from.' She spoke the words with less of an impending sense of doom than she had managed before now. *In fact*, she thought, *I feel better for telling him*.

'Yes,' he mused. 'Perhaps you would allow me to examine the skin wounds again tonight before Joanie covers them in salve.'

Melissa drew a startled breath. Her uninjured eye opened wide, and she wondered whether her mouth did not drop open, too, as Joanie's had done last night.

'Well, ma'am, you do not forbid it.' The colonel rose and took his seat once more. Melissa realised she was clasping his handkerchief, but merely squeezed it as tightly as her injured right hand would permit. His gaze went to the action. 'Your arm has only minor scarring, but the hand is clearly incapacitated,' he observed. 'I know you were rescued from the house in Great Russell Street. Did you suffer broken bones?'

'My right arm was broken in two places, and I only removed the splint the day before yesterday. Perhaps you think this is too early?' She wanted to know what he thought. Suddenly, his opinion was very important.

'Maybe, but we could try a sling instead of the splint, if you would permit Zed and myself to work on it. His assistance is invaluable to me.' The question felt like a test of some kind, and that her future relations with

Colonel Henry Gunn depended on the answer she gave.

Melissa quailed. She'd endured so much intrusion. So many folk had examined and touched her since the fire that the thought of undergoing yet more was daunting. And Zed was not a physician that she knew of, although what did she know of either of these self-assured men? One thing was certain: it was only eight weeks since her accident, and her body was not healed.

She nodded.

Chaos erupted downstairs. Raised voices competed with running feet, and the colonel was up and across to the door in seconds. Joanie darted to the window and looked out onto the carriage drive.

'It's a coach, your ladyship, and there's . . . ' She nearly choked on the realisation of what she was seeing. ' . . . there's the other one.' Melissa watched the girl's terrified eyes swivel to Harry Gunn's sharp glare. 'You've tricked us,' the maid breathed as she came to stand behind her. Melissa felt a comforting pressure on her good shoulder.

Gunn brought a hand up to his brow. The look he sent Melissa was full of despair, and it was seconds before he was able to bring it under control.

'The other one? Do you mean Colonel Gunn's *distant* cousin, George?' Melissa struggled to keep her voice calm and modulated and was quite pleased with the result. Her heart, however, thumped its own misery in her chest. What a fool she'd been to allow this man to seduce her with his pleasing manner and gentle hands.

Behind her, she felt Joanie straighten, and knew the girl would be nodding. Her strong fingers dug into Melissa's shoulder before she let go.

'So, Colonel Gunn, how has this come about? Please, if you can manage it, do not lie to me.' Her words whipped across the room like a lash,

43

and she saw Gunn cringe. Good. What was this all about?

'I don't know, ma'am. Truly, I am as horrified as you must be.' He sent his sharp gaze around the room, but there was no prospect of an escape onto a secondary staircase. They could hear an argument already starting between Zed and a well-bred female. 'This room is unusual with its windows on two sides, but of course that means it is the last room on the corridor.'

The door was flung wide, and a small compact version of Harry Gunn advanced into the room. George came behind her at a more sedate pace, and Zed brought up the rear of the procession in injured silence.

'Lottie,' Harry Gunn said; and to Melissa it sounded strained. 'You must have already been on the road from Lauder before our instructions reached you.'

'And how good it is to see you, too, Harry,' the woman said in barely suppressed fury. 'George brings me news of a seriously injured friend of the family, and I drop everything to speed here to assist you — and that's your welcome.'

'My dear, forgive me,' he apologised; and moving forward, took his sister in his arms and held her tightly to him.

'All right, all right. No need to squeeze the life out of me. You must be Lady Pateley, ma'am. I am so very honoured to make your acquaintance. Harry, introduce me to the countess without your usual delay.' The woman escaped from Gunn's grip and came to stand in front of Melissa.

Melissa did not rise, but studied the visitor from her seat on the sofa. The new arrival was not above five feet in height, and yet her presence filled the room, making the other occupants dim. She wore a warm pelisse in dark grey, and under it Melissa saw a woollen travelling dress in paler shades, perhaps dove, she thought. *Why am I taking so much notice of this?* she wondered. *Do I hope to*

45

divert myself from Gunn's treachery?

'Lady Pateley, may I present my sister, Mrs Fraser Duart. In the family we call her Lottie.' The colonel spoke in his usual measured tones, but Melissa heard hesitation there.

Goodness, I've been less than a day in his company and I pretend to read his moods.

'Lady Pateley.' The woman was extending her hand, and Melissa began to raise hers in response, but was stopped by a bark from the colonel.

'Lottie! Have a care, can't you. Lady Pateley's arm will not withstand your attentions.'

Melissa saw the chagrin flash through the older woman's eyes and was sorry for it. Gunn's sister had come full tilt to offer the protection of her name to a stranger, and she was shouted at.

'I regret your brother is in the right of this, ma'am. My arm was broken when I fell through the house in the fire. I only had the splint off recently, and it does not yet cope as it once did.'

Melissa tried to smile, but she was finding dissimulation such as the colonel was practising had deserted her. 'I am, however, very pleased to make your acquaintance. There is a paucity of women in my current company and an accompanying lack of sense.'

'Good afternoon, Melissa,' George spoke. He had moved silently across the Paxtons' many rugs, and studied Melissa and Mrs Duart as if they were a tableau.

Melissa felt chill. Did he practise to make his tone without a shiver of expression? she wondered. If so, he'd had a good master. She did not reply and did not cast so much as a glance in the man's direction.

This family may think they will break my spirit, but it has been through fire and it is tempered by the dreadful Withershaws in ways they cannot understand.

Why is Henry Gunn so subdued in his relatives' company?

Mrs Duart seemed nonplussed by

47

her silence, but Melissa caught a gleam of understanding in the depths of her hazel eyes. *No,* she thought in irritation, *she sees attachment where none exists. She thinks I'm pretending I do not know him.*

'I am sorry to be so forceful, Lady Pateley. George is our cousin, and when he outlined the horror of your recent history, I could not but suggest Harry might bring you here, as I know he and Thomas Paxton are still as thick as schoolboys in their friendship. Naturally, I invited George to join me. I understand . . . ' She glanced darkly at Joanie, but clearly the excitement of what she thought she understood was greater than her fear of what servants might or might not know. ' . . . from George that you have been hounded by persons investigating your husband's death and the fire and even your personal circumstances. He continues to be most anxious to offer his assistance.'

'Mrs Duart . . . '

'Please, ma'am, do call me Lottie.'

'Lottie, I have been travelling; and if Colonel Gunn's men have prepared some rooms, I would retire.'

Ignoring Lottie's puzzlement over her bad manners, Melissa stood. George started to come even closer, but Harry was there in an instant and offered her his right arm once more. She was tempted to ignore that, too, but was shaking so much realised she might collapse without his support and slipped her uninjured left arm under his elbow. Did that allow him to measure the tremors passing through her? He stooped and lifted her off her feet.

'Quietly, my lady, I think it best.'

'Do you ever think in any other way?' she asked, but in truth being in his arms for the moment was the best answer. George could not reach her here.

* * *

Harry strode across the saloon and onto the landing. Joanie was at his heels and Zed at hers. Having asked his sister to attend him here, it made a poor showing of hospitality, but he needed to get Melissa Pateley away from George.

'Zed?'

'One floor up, Colonel. There are two rooms the ladies will be most comfortable in, and Mistress Paxton has left everything in order.' Zed pushed round the maid more gently than his earlier behaviour and advanced to a short flight of stairs. He nipped up, and Harry followed more slowly, carrying the countess.

She weighs very little. I hope that does not indicate any problems with her guts. The trembling is lessening as we leave George behind. I wish my own over Lottie's anger would do the same.

'In here, sir.' Zed indicated a door, and it led into a large chamber flooded with late-afternoon sun. Harry crossed towards the tester bed, and when Joanie had pulled back the top covers, lowered the countess into it. He felt the power of her gaze as he brought his head up and needed every ounce of courage he could summon to hold her stare.

'I think you may sleep comfortably, ma'am. It may seem a bad pass, and I regret my sister's impulsive action, but sometimes it can be wise to hold your enemies close.' It sounded a feeble excuse for the personification of his guest's worst nightmare, but what else could he say? he wondered.

'Mrs Duart was awaiting your word?' Melissa asked.

'She was. We knew we were likely to find you in Berwick Old Abbey because we'd followed a trail and tested all the other properties owned by your estate except it and The Burnside.' He lifted the bedclothes and drew them across the girl before she shivered. 'I am embarrassed to find George was so close without any of my scouts discovering him.'

'Then you may not know George as well as I,' she said; and Harry watched her eyelids flutter closed and open again. She was on the brink of

51

exhaustion, and his presence was not helping her now. 'I could have told you how close that devil would be.'

'You must sleep. Joanie, too. There's a truckle bed for her which she should pull across the door. I will have a detail on the landing outside.' He stood away and let the young maid take his place. As he and Zed left, they heard the countess murmur from sleep.

'He brought that devil back. Will no one relieve me?'

'What do we make of it, sir?' Zed asked as they stood for a moment, taking stock.

'I'm damned if I know, man, but he does not sleep under this roof. I'm not breaking bread with him.' Harry's hand went to his waist, although he'd taken his sword off earlier and he found nothing there. 'My great uncle was explicit. George is a danger to the countess and would bring scandal on the family if allowed to get too close.'

'But why?' Zed was as puzzled as Harry had been. Now he thought he saw what his estranged cousin was about, and he hated it.

'We have seen much odd behaviour on our travels, have we not? I begin to think my cousin has an obsession with this young woman. I begin to think he would own her soul if he could.' Harry turned back as if he would enter the room again.

'Own her soul, sir? Not just wed her and take the money?'

Harry shook his head. Military tactics were so much less difficult to work out than the machinations of a madman. What did he mean by his behaviour? George had always been looked askance by the older members of the family, but Uncle John had been emphatic and agitated when he spoke to Harry.

'I hate to say it. I hate to give credence to the rumours that flew about when his papa was locked away, but I must. The girl needs our protection, and you are the only one able to command sufficient men to do it. You must snatch her.' The elderly gentleman had taken a long draw on his pipe before calming himself sufficiently to go on. 'His papa was taken while stealing into the rooms of a duke's daughter. He'd previously been warned off over and over, and even the girl's impending marriage did not deter him. I see George with the same unnerving disregard for this young woman's humanity.'

Harry had not shared this conversation with Zed or any of his sisters. Now he wondered what they did next. Uncle John had hoped removing Lady Pateley from view would dampen George's ardour or possibly divert his attentions elsewhere. It had been no part of their plans to have him under the same roof as the injured countess.

3

'You must not be surprised, Harry.' Lottie's sharp tone alerted Harry to the sure sense he had failed again. Why did it take no more than an hour to force him back into his childhood role of bumbling uselessness? 'George has gone.'

'What!' Wrath exploded, enveloping him and bringing his sister's interested gaze to his no doubt blazing complexion. 'What do you mean, Lottie? How could you allow him to depart without alerting me or Zed?'

Lottie sent a glance of mildly tolerant humour towards his steward and right-hand man before turning back. 'Well, as to that, young sir, you seemed to be closeted in the countess's bedroom, and neither George nor I were allowed up even the first pair of stairs. It really isn't good enough.'

'George tried to come up?' Harry asked, but it was more or less what he would have expected, and did expect, and had set guards to prevent.

'He came here with the lady's welfare close to his heart, and yet she did not acknowledge him; and you, his cousin and head of the family, did not acknowledge him. How could he linger on when his honour was so impugned?' Lottie spread the folds of her travelling dress with steady hands. Harry knew that running her own establishment had only confirmed her belief in the rightness of her opinions. All of her opinions, however ill-advised.

'Tis a small enough wonder Fraser Duart spends so much time in Siam. If I were him, I'd think it only far enough distant.

'Lottie, I could not write everything about this mission . . . '

'Ah, I wondered when it would all take on a military flavour. Still playing soldiers are we? At thirty-two, Harry? Where are my mother's heirs?' Lottie twisted the conversation back to her, and therefore in her mind the family's, favourite topic.

'Lottie, please desist.' Harry spoke with just enough of the commander to make his sister listen for once. 'I would have told you much more of the story had you arrived alone as I requested.'

'George is family.' The degree of outrage Lottie managed to imbue into her words was enough to defeat Harry temporarily. He had made a mistake in seeking her help, and regretted not pressing on to Edinburgh and the house in George Square he now occupied there. His mama lived in his household. It would be easy to accommodate the countess without compromising her.

'George's father was also family. Would you have brought him along?'

'I never met the man. I have heard uncle John prose on about his failings. As if every great family did not have its share of eccentric cousins.' Lottie stood and paced a little. It never failed to catch Harry by surprise the way his sister's nature leant to the energetic. 'You should remember, sir, mere females are kept out of much of what their male relatives engage in.'

'I do remember it. I am telling you now. George Gunn is an embarrassment to our name and a danger to Lady Pateley.'

'Telling me? You are yelling, Harry. Loudness does not add verisimilitude to unsound reasoning. I keep explaining that to my own brood.' Lottie sat down again. 'I have instructed your cook-man to serve dinner at five of the clock. Were *you* to instruct the guards, I would retire to my room for an hour.'

'Lottie, I beg pardon. I do not mean to yell, and I will try to remember your sensible observations. However, George is not a maligned person with good intentions. He has been pursuing Lady Pateley relentlessly, and I have only just managed to keep one step ahead of him.' Harry saw his sister's shoulders stiffen and knew he'd lost the argument for the present. It was always thus when they were younger and she had assumed his upbringing during an extended period of illness their mama suffered. He would have to come at her again when he could think of a different approach.

'Five o'clock will be excellent. Zed, please see Mrs Duart to her room.'

* * *

Melissa glanced at the tin bath resting on a rug before the fireplace. The fire was not lit, and she could listen to pigeons cooing far above on the chimney pot. She stood up and began to cross the bedroom, but her legs threatened to buckle, and Joanie slipped a stool behind her so she could sit.

'This is a result of that man's intrusion in our habits,' she said bitterly. 'I was walking well until two nights ago.'

'You're still groggy from sleeping at an odd time of day, my lady, and you didn't eat a lot of the food they sent up.' Joanie clucked like an old hen and Melissa had to bite back a sharper retort than the girl deserved. How would she have survived even the first day after the fire without Simmerton, Joanie and Percy? she constantly reminded herself. It did give them certain rights, or let them think they had certain rights.

'You haven't eaten much,' a male voice said behind her, and Melissa knew it was not Simmerton or Percy. In fact, there was a tingling sensation down the left side of her head that had told her Harry Gunn was in the room before he opened his mouth.

'I tried,' she said. 'Perhaps once I've been awake for an hour or so, I might do better.' She glanced round and saw a vision of male beauty that would have caused widespread swooning in Almack's rooms. Harry Gunn was dressed in a dark blue tail coat and linen so white, Melissa thought it dazzled. His pantaloons stretched tight across thighs that looked as if they too were tailored, or at least cut, from marble cloth.

'You changed for the meal?' she asked, and wondered if it really sounded peevish. Why did she resent missing the chance of dining with this misguided colonel?

'My older sister expects standards to be kept up, even in the depths of the countryside with no one else present.' Melissa heard again the slightly defensive tone Harry adopted when talking with or about his sister. It was puzzling to think that the young man who'd been promoted twice on the battlefield was daunted by that petite brunette.

'Of course, Mrs Duart.'

'And Zed. George Gunn has gone.'

Melissa's heart stopped. It kicked in again, and she clung to the sides of the stool. How had she forgotten?

'Gone?' she asked, raising wide eyes to the colonel. 'Gone where, and why?'

She watched Harry Gunn's face and knew with a sickening dread that he could not answer her. George had done what he was so good at — always.

'I think I see, Colonel. As soon as his plans are thwarted, he disappears and plots some more and then turns up again with a fresh one.' She knew her voice was full of bitterness, but could do nothing to erase it. George Gunn had been doing this for months now, and some even believed he had a right to be with her; a right to intrude in her life. She wondered if he was someone's puppet. His regular disappearing acts were executed so cleanly, it was as if he could not wait to take himself out of the firing line.

'This, I surmise, has been his way. My sister . . . '

'Could have done nothing other than what she did. On a first meeting, I would have fallen for George's platitudes myself — and did do so once, or perhaps twice.' She shuddered and caught sight of the steward, Zed, testing the temperature of her bath. It brought her back into the present with an unpleasant jolt.

'I have not yet bathed,' she said, and glanced at Gunn. 'Perhaps you and Zed would leave us now.'

The silence in the room was fragile and soon broken. Joanie's laboured breathing competed with the pigeons on the chimney, and Harry Gunn tapped a toe rhythmically against the leg of a chair. Her injured eye slid closed, but her good one drowned in the hazel depths of Harry Gunn's regard.

'I think, ma'am, we reached an agreement earlier about your future treatment,' he said at last, and Melissa quailed. 'I am loath to force our attentions on you when you are used to the best London physicians, but we are also good — '

'At resuscitating men to fight on,' she snapped, driven beyond politeness to defend herself with her tongue. She had no other weapons where this man was concerned.

'Ma'am, do not — '

'What? Defend my right to privacy

for my scarred and injured body? Do you think I don't know about the learned papers some have written describing it?' Melissa shuddered again.

Joanie had cut off her hair after the fire when so much of it had been frizzled by burning cloth, and there was no satisfying toss of shining locks as she defied the man trying to help her. Pateley would have hated it. Her mass of chestnut ringlets had been her husband's joy.

'I only married you, my beautiful strumpet, for the right to run my hands through this.' Melissa felt the threat of tears and redoubled her anger. She had done enough crying to last a lifetime.

'Lady Pateley, I am sorry for what the science of medicine has put you through, but Zed and I are skilled practitioners and we will not be writing up your case in any journal or popular paper. There were many battles, and you must realise my rank is senior for my age. Thomas Paxton is nigh on fifty and only bought his commission ten years ago.'

Melissa knew from newspaper reports and the talk among Pateley's friends that Henry Gunn had earned promotion on the battlefield. She had assumed it was for numbers killed. Perhaps though, there was another explanation.

'You mean, sir, your promotions in the field were for numbers saved?'

'We begin to understand one another, I hope, ma'am. Of course, the patients in the field are men, but several among the camp followers were hurt or suffered dangerous deliveries in labour. We are able to say that the female body is known to us both.' Harry Gunn was stripping off his coat, and when Melissa looked to the bath, she saw Zed had already taken his off. He was unravelling a roll of clean white cotton and tossed a length to Gunn, who tied it around his clothing like a large apron.

★ ★ ★

The men had found a screen some-where, and now Melissa watched them set it around the bath. It had paintings of Chinese characters on two of the panels, and huge white birds that might be cranes on the central one. Clearly, she thought, Agnes Paxton was a woman of good taste.

'Zed and I will wait while your maid assists with your bath. He's already added some herbs to it, and I have brought this soap,' the colonel addressed her, and she nodded, too overcome by the oddness of her circumstances to say anything. He handed the soap to Joanie before helping her to her feet and supporting her across the room. Zed brought the stool and she sank down again.

'Why am I more enfeebled tonight? I was making some progress with walking and using my arm . . . ' Tears once more threatened to overcome her and she trailed off into silence. How different her life was from the vibrancy of the early months of her marriage. In those days, she would have seen off George Gunn with ease and made sure the lawyers were working for her and not against her.

'It is not unusual for a person to relapse when another shock visits them.' The quiet words soothed her agitation. This man believed she was not a hopeless case, and that was worth knowing.

Melissa waited while the men retreated around the screen, then rose slowly to undress and step carefully into the water. She and Joanie managed to wash off the dirt of travelling and sleeping out of doors and some of the dried salve. It was twenty-four hours since it had last been applied and had crusted in places.

'My lady, I am sorry. Here, I'll soak this cloth, and that might help to soften the crustiness.' Joanie dropped the square of muslin she was using into the cooling water and then set it on the worst of the residue for a moment or two.

'Do not rub the surfaces, Joanie,' Harry Gunn said from behind the screen, and the women looked at each other.

He's been following everything we've done by listening in. Truly, he might as well be round here with me.

'I think we've finished, my lady,' Joanie said very quietly, and Melissa knew the girl was wondering what would happen next. She was herself, but her self-appointed physician had no such hesitation.

'Joanie, please assist Lady Pateley to stand out of the bath. You should then wrap her in the towels.' Joanie sent Melissa a glance full of such outrage, she laughed a little.

'It's all right, Joanie. We've come this far, and the injuries have responded well, but we have run out of expertise. The colonel and his man have seen and treated so many more examples.' Melissa was glad of Joanie's strong grip as she balanced on one leg to lift the other over the rim of the tub. How had they managed when she was first injured?

'I think it will be best, ma'am, if I carry you over to the bed,' Harry Gunn said; and with this second of warning he came around the screen and scooped Melissa into his arms. Joanie fluttered around trying to keep the towelling decently wrapped, but Melissa suspected she was only partly successful.

The colonel had an antiseptic smell and his hands were stained a brownish-purple. When Melissa caught sight of Zed's hands, she saw they, too, had turned the same unattractive colour. While she was bathing, the men had stripped back her bedclothes and placed several thicknesses of cotton on the bottom sheets. Harry Gunn laid her gently down on this.

'Now, ma'am, I would like you to turn onto your left side, please.'

Melissa turned over, with some difficulty and not a little pain and lay face down under the towels. She heard Joanie's shocked gasp as the colonel eased the towels away. He was silent for several moments, and then he and Zed stood away from the bed to hold a muted conference. He came back and spoke softly to her.

'We think your treatment so far has been good, ma'am, and Joanie has been careful to spread the apothecary's salve all the way over the exposed and healing skin. What we propose to do now is start using a different salve, one we developed out on the battlefield to treat canonball burns and the after-effects of explosions.' As he spoke, the colonel smoothed salve like a thick cream over her, and Melissa began to feel drowsy. 'Do not sleep, please. We need to look at your arm tonight.'

All too soon, the men had stood away to allow Joanie to help her don a thick chemise and sit up on the edge of the bed. The stained cloth was removed and the two men undid their makeshift aprons.

Colonel Gunn gave her a wry smile as they turned back to her. 'This is

Zed's speciality, and I'm sorry to say, he can make battle-hardened soldiers faint.'

'I think you might have more patients if you did not tell them before the procedure that it will be so painful,' Melissa protested.

'Very few of them had a choice, and of course your injury is now set, so he will not be manipulating the bones. We hope.' The colonel drew a hand through his hair, and Melissa thought she could see sweat forming on his brow.

'Don't listen to him, Lady Pateley. He has been known to faint himself, and that's what concerns him. I will not be re-breaking your arm,' Zed said laconically. Melissa felt his hands grip her right arm and carefully stroke it from the shoulder down to the elbow. Then he cradled her forearm and gently probed it all the way to the wrist.

'Well?' Gunn asked.

'A good job, I believe, Colonel. I would have manipulated the break in the forearm a little more to the right, but I think her ladyship will regain most of her previous capability.' Zed stood away. He held Melissa's gaze with a patient smile, and she found herself smiling back at him.

'Perhaps you should have been a physician, Zed, and not a soldier.'

'Perhaps, ma'am. I would have liked it, but then I would not have had the chance to learn from the colonel here.' Zed bowed and, turning abruptly, left the bedroom.

'I did not intend to give offence, Colonel,' she said. The manipulation of her arm had left her exhausted, but she was concerned in case the man had misunderstood her. She knew how painful it was to be misjudged. Withershaws had made sure of that.

'I do not believe Zed will have taken any. He started life in the Poor's House, an institution much like the Foundling Hospital in London. We know nothing about his antecedents, and I think he does find that hard when his skills are pointed up.' Harry Gunn kept his hazel gaze fixed on her face, and she knew he was assessing how she had been affected by their examinations.

'Will you please tell me what thoughts are troubling you?' she asked at last.

'I had hoped we might move on tomorrow and reach my house in Edinburgh, but we have depleted your strength and that will not be possible.' He moved away, and Melissa felt bereft.

'I think you are right about that, if not about removing me from my sanctuary in the first place.'

A shadow crossed his face, but he recovered quickly and made a wry grimace. 'Tactics are always a closely argued subject, ma'am. We will discuss my actions when you are more rested. Good night.'

Melissa made an attempt to eat a little more of the cold meat and fresh vegetables sent up by Harry Gunn's cook, but knew she was falling asleep. Joanie took the trays and left the room.

Alone in the gathering dark of a

Scottish country evening, she tried to find solace in familiar sounds. When they were married first, Pateley had brought her to his hunting box in the English Borders. It was across the river Tweed and not many miles from where she thought the Keep of Duns might be situated.

Her husband had introduced her to lying still and listening. Like a blanket, silence creeps over one but soon it is broken. Early on, owls hoot. Their eerie cries may warn their prey, but soon there are screeches and wails that testify to their hunting skills. Bats stream out of the roof spaces, and an occasional one enters the darkening room to circle in increasing panic and puzzlement.

The wind soughs among the trees, and if it rises, then a branch may be heard breaking off. As it tumbles earthwards, other smaller branches crash and clatter and an occasional small animal squeals.

Storms blow up out of nowhere and bring swaths of rain. In summer, fire flares in the deep woods when lightning has found a target.

Or in the centre of civilisation, when a house is dried out by drought, lightning spares no one and nothing in its path. It burns, burns with intensity until the pain makes you cry out, and . . .

'You are safe, my lady.'

'No, the fire. We must run. Joanie, catch me . . . '

'You are safe. Here, I have you. Lie still.'

And Melissa lay still. When she woke in the early light, she was alone.

4

Melissa lowered herself down the main stairs of the absent Thomas Paxton's house and stood for a moment or two. It was quiet, and only the chiming of a clock somewhere told her the morning was advancing towards midday.

'Eleven o'clock,' she murmured, and stopped. The tiny hairs on her scalp shivered. Harry Gunn was behind her.

'Good morning, ma'am,' he said. 'My sister has just risen from the breakfast table, and she and her maid are taking a turn around the vegetable gardens.' He put a hand below her elbow when she turned too quickly and her balance deserted her. He smiled, but kept his hold.

'Oh. Mrs Duart does not enjoy vistas?' Melissa wondered why the lady would choose to go there first. She was confident that anyone who kept such an elegant house as Mrs Paxton would also have retained the most fashionable landscape artist to instil order into her outdoors.

'Lottie is married to a plant collector and knows a great deal more than she would ever allow on early acquaintance about plants, trees and vistas. However, she is temporary chatelaine of this house, and my staff and has gone to interview Paxton's head gardener.'

'You give me the impression that you wish she would not be the temporary chatelaine of your staff at the least,' Melissa said; and for the first time in many months felt a gurgle of laughter rise within her. She was pleased to see Harry Gunn respond with a laugh of his own.

'Come, there is still breakfast,' he said, although she noticed he did not respond to her mild sally about his sister and urged her towards a door leading from the downstairs hall. 'I rang for fresh coffee when Zed reported you were on your way downstairs.'

'I dislike being watched so closely, sir. I have managed to get up and down the staircase in my own home for at least two weeks.' Melissa knew it was a forceful protest over such a small point, but the words were out before she could stop them.

'Of course you have, but the last two days have been full of unnecessary strain and fresh challenges like sleeping in the open air.' He paused. She wondered whether he was waiting a little for her to mention the thing that was undoubtedly puzzling her, but she turned her head away in case he saw the flash of recognition in her good eye.

Surely I dreamed I fell asleep with his arms around me. And his breath whispering in my ear. And his long legs trapping mine so I did not thrash around and throw off the bedclothes once more.

'Strain. Yes, I have felt extra strain, although I slept well in the outdoors and last night, too — after a bit of time.' She looked round the breakfast room and breathed in the smells of civilisation. Warm meaty smells mingled with coffee and the pollen from a huge vase of lilies placed in the hearth. 'I dreamed that someone gathered me close and chased away the nightmare.'

Harry Gunn held a chair for her and eased it under her as she sat down. She realised they were not entirely alone as she had first thought when a youngish man with an empty left sleeve set a plate of food in front of her. He was smartly dressed in a suit of hard-wearing material that was not quite a livery. Melissa turned her head and smiled into mischievous blue eyes.

'The colonel said as how you'd be hungry, my lady,' the young man said, and Melissa was enchanted. This was no starchy footman engaged from a registry of servants, but a returning soldier who probably had several adoring female relatives in his home village.

'Thank you. I am, and the enticing

smell your cook has made me more so,' Melissa answered, although she knew a high-born lady would not have responded to the young man's breach of protocol. His colour flared, and he turned away to bring some floury rolls, and set the basket beside Melissa. She was reaching towards them when the door opened again.

'If you've finished gawking,' Mrs Duart said from the threshold; and Melissa caught Harry Gunn's sharp intake of breath. The young footman, if that was what he was, was unabashed.

'Thank you, ma'am. The colonel asked me to remain in position, as Lady Pateley's own personal footmen, Percy and Matt, are helping her maid and butler to unpack and repack their boxes.'

'Harry!'

Melissa could wait no longer and lifted her fork to attack the steaming arrangement of mushrooms and eggs on her plate. She had already given Mrs Duart cause to think she had few manners worth the calling and knew if she did not satisfy her hunger soon, she would add bad temper to that catalogue. Even so, she was interested in her host's reaction.

I call him host, and yet really, the man is my abductor.

'Harry, surely there are servants' registries in Edinburgh or Newcastle that would supply the names of properly trained young persons with characters?' Mrs Duart asked; but as she appeared to have no interest in her brother's answer, carried on before he could frame any kind of reply. 'Servants who remember their place among their employers are silent.'

'Sorry, ma'am,' the boy said, compounding everything that had gone before, 'but those are my orders from the colonel.'

'Out!'

Melissa felt there must be an exchange of glances between her helper and the colonel, but she kept her head bent lest Mrs Duart decide invalids should subsist on gruel. The food was delicious, and she knew if she could just have one of those rolls spread with country butter and the honey dripping off a spoon she could see across the table, then life would be looking much better than it had done for some time. From trying to lift one earlier, she knew the spreading of it was not something her injured right hand would be able to do yet.

'Mrs Duart, I wonder whether you would oblige me by spreading one of those rolls with butter and honey, please?' Melissa turned towards Lottie Duart, whose face had set in a rigid grimace as her welcoming smile turned to horror.

The young footman moved back to the table and with calm competence lifted a roll from the basket. They'd already been sliced, and he set it onto a small plate where he trapped it under the edge of another small plate. He spread butter and then dripped honey in a golden stream onto the roll.

'I see I will be able to take lessons from you ... What is your name?' Melissa smiled at the footman as she accepted the bread.

'Donal, my lady. Will ye be wanting anything else?'

'Thank you, Donal; I think the colonel will pour me coffee.'

She acknowledged Donal's tight little bow and watched as he crossed to the door. Lottie Duart's maid sprang to life and opened it for him, but he glared down at her as if she'd physically assaulted him. Melissa understood that look.

'Well!' Lottie said before sinking into a chair. Neither Melissa, whose mouth was full of bread, nor Harry, who looked as if he'd seen the family ghost, replied. 'I do beg your pardon, Lady Pateley, but I have been examining the carrots and my hands are a little muddy.'

Melissa glanced sideways and saw that this was in fact the case. Lottie was mud-stained.

'No need to apologise, Mrs Duart . . .'

'Please, Lottie. I find in the family circle, first names are the most comfortable.'

Melissa opened her left eye wide at the strength of Lottie's smile. Her right opened a little, but was again watering copiously, and she soon let the lid flutter over it. This was a moment of decision, she knew. Would she accept Lottie's friendship, or was she, too, an abductor?

Across the table, Harry Gunn was still mute, and the camaraderie of their first few moments was gone. She watched his hand pick at the table linen and wondered whether he would succeed in creating a hole. There was an issue between him and this sister who had acted as his mother, that much was clear. Did she want to exploit it? She swallowed the last bite of roll and honey and sent a longing gaze towards the basket.

'Lottie, of course; and I hope you will use my own given name. It's Melissa.'

84

'I expect that's why you are so enamoured of the honey,' Harry Gunn said as he removed her plate and replaced it with another bearing a second roll generously spread and neatly cut into four quarters. 'We find honey is a valuable commodity in our work as well as being delicious.'

'Harry, you do go on. I trust Lady Pateley is being attended as soon as possible in Edinburgh by one of my mama's favourite physicians,' Lottie interrupted her brother. 'It's all very well for you and that Zed man to pretend to knowledge, but they have the parchment that proves theirs.'

'I have been seen by several men with parchments,' Melissa said, 'and none of them have made me feel as recovering as I do this morning.'

'No?' Lottie sat with her handsome head slightly tilted and her huge hazel eyes that were so like her brother's wide in amazement. 'However, Harry and his aide-de-camp come along after the others, do not they? Their ministrations are late in the process.'

'Why, I find that remark to be ungenerous,' Melissa said with more of a snap than she had exhibited for weeks. 'Besides, who has decided I will be travelling to Edinburgh?'

The question brought about a rare moment of agreement between the siblings, and Melissa was aware of the glances they exchanged, although she only had the one eye with which to observe them at present. She noticed that Harry recovered first, and he stood up in agitation.

'There is no alternative, ma'am. George does not have the use of men in the way I do, but he is able to sneak about.'

Melissa heard Lottie's sharp intake of breath, although she kept her gaze fixed on Harry Gunn for the moment.

'You said so yourself, last night.'

She remembered some troubled words escaping her as she drifted into sleep and knew well they might have been something to that effect about her tormentor. 'And perhaps I did, Colonel, because the man turns up in places where he has no right nor obligation.' That word brought Melissa's thoughts into sharp relief. 'It still mystifies me why you think you have any duty to protect me.'

'Goodness, that's easily answered, and I'm surprised you haven't worked it out, ma'am.' Lottie's sharp tongue crackled with irritation. 'Harry is wont to lumber himself, the family and our estates with as many lame and halt as he can . . .'

'I think, Lottie, we must see the parting of our ways,' Harry said. His chill tone was laced with fury, and Melissa could understand why. How had the woman forgotten the extent and severity of her injuries? If any was lame and halt, it was herself.

'I beg your pardon, Lady Pateley. I know your circumstances do not make you any kind of burden in the ways I outlined. I was referring solely to the likes of the young man who served you breakfast.' Lottie drew breath, but neither of them could use the interval to interrupt her flow. 'Why should he be kept on when there are any number of clansmen in need of employment?'

'So there we have it, Lottie. Because Donal's name is Campbell and not Gunn, he must go back to a hovel in a hamlet and starve.'

'He will have people of his own to look after him,' the woman protested warmly. 'This is why we need to look after Lady Pateley.'

Melissa looked at her with interest. Her nerves were alert to the changing tenor of her voice and the rather arch expression she was assuming.

'If she and George are to be married . . . '

Melissa stood, too, then and sent Lottie a blazing glance. 'I will never marry your cousin.'

'Oh, ma'am, I know it is scarcely two months since the fire in London, but you have been a widow for nearly three years and must long for the comfort of a husband and settled home.'

'Must I, though?' Melissa burned with the force of her anger. 'I am not so lost for company and friends that I wish to be married to anyone who offers at any cost.'

'My cousin . . . '

'Is not and never will be a contender for my hand,' Melissa also interrupted Lottie Duart. 'You would do well to think very carefully before doing anything, anything at all to promote his suit.'

She turned towards the door, and Harry Gunn was there before her, pulling it open. His glance was full of a compassion that was nearly her undoing, and she left without a backward glance.

★ ★ ★

'That was unforgiveable, Lottie.' Harry closed the door on the countess and turned back to his sister. He could not bring himself to meet her gaze, but levelled his own on her maid. The girl made a swift curtsey and disappeared through a door beside the fireplace. Harry hoped it led onto a passage and was not simply a large cupboard.

'I could have phrased it more sweetly, perhaps,' Lottie said. He heard the words, but he'd heard many similar platitudes over the years. She was giving ground only to make an over-powering rush when she felt her opponent's defences were lowered.

'Or not said anything at all.' He moved around Thomas and Agnes's parlour, glancing at the array of ornaments and wondering at the number of pieces of china Agnes had managed to accumulate.

'That would no doubt suit you better than to have the whole family silently seething over your dissipation of the estate.' Lottie was watching him from across the table and he saw her strong gardener's fingers moving back and forth across its board. 'You must see that as you are blindly committed to playing at a profession you have no qualifications for and supporting men who are being kept from their own clans by your actions. George's marriage to the countess would restore funds to our coffers.'

'Did you discuss this with him?' Harry asked in mounting horror. Surely Lottie did not believe George had any intention of helping the family cause?

'No, but he made it plain he had loved the woman for many months and was prepared to wed her despite her injuries. When he has, then her fortune may be spent wisely on behalf of the family. It's not as if she has any of her own, is it?' Lottie summed up her argument with the kind of unanswerable fact she was fond of parading.

'I wonder if you have been neglecting your garden in favour of reading the scandal sheets, my dear.' Harry knew Melissa Pateley did have family, although some of them had been displeased by her early marriage to a cash-strapped aristocrat. No doubt a lot of Flaxxe revenue had gone into restoring Neville Pateley's decaying estate.

'You do not contradict me with facts, Harry.'

'I have never found facts to make the slightest headway with your view of the world. I must ask you to depart. The countess is too frail as yet to make the journey to Edinburgh . . . '

'Then you will need me here to give you countenance,' Lottie interrupted. 'Although the lady is a widow, her reputation would not be enhanced by an extended stay in an isolated country house with a bachelor.'

Harry heard the venom his sister imbued the word with, and it squeezed his heart. He had been to the point of offering for a lady on occasion, but something had always intervened to forestall the words. Certainly time was passing, and the moment when he needed to think of the succession as laird was becoming pressing. But he had two younger sisters in rude health and settled in good marriages. The name might not continue, but the responsibilities would be looked after by another generation. It was his position as only son that infused Lottie with so much irritation.

'We must take our chance with the gossip-mongers, I'm afraid. You insulted the countess and you insulted every injured soldier who relies on me for employment.' Harry did look at her then, and was surprised a flash of fear. It was quickly suppressed.

'You keep them from their clans.'

'No, Lottie, I do not. They have all made at least one visit home. Four or five send some wages to their mothers. The majority were welcome for a week or two in their homelands, but soon learned they were eating food grown by younger brothers and came back to Auchenwylde.' Harry rubbed a hand across his brow. They did come back, those injured men with bewilderment in their eyes and dread in their hearts.

'And you have them making soap,' Lottie said.

'Yes.' His answer was short. Lottie had no interest in the qualities of the soap they produced or the way work and food changed damaged men into less damaged.

'Soap, not even Uisge Beatha.'

'I try to keep them sober. I am not going to argue my decisions with you, Lottie. You must go up to George Square and keep your counsel, if you please, else I may insist you return to Duart's clan on Mull.'

'The island life does not always suit me, and I find that when Fraser is travelling, his mama becomes a little demanding of my time.' She stood up. 'Very well, I see your mind is made up. But remember, Harry — the family agrees with me.'

Harry wondered whether they did, and if so about what. Certainly they had all been guilty of allowing Lottie to trample them with her forceful words and busy personality.

5

When Melissa left the breakfast parlour, the door closed behind her, and she stopped. The shock of Lottie's attack was live in her mind like the flashes of pain she'd suffered when the burns were fresh. She leant against the wall and breathed slowly until her balance righted and she could move without that fear of falling over which she'd lived with for weeks.

'My lady, are you quite well?'

Melissa looked across the hall and saw Donal pushing a makeshift barrow loaded with a laundry basket. The vision of a steaming bath rose unwanted in her mind.

He saw everything and yet it did not make him blench.

'Yes; I was dizzy, but I'm able to move again now. Is your band of men very large?' she asked, and saw how the young man coloured beneath her scrutiny. 'Ah, I am to be told nothing of the arrangements.'

'The colonel's orders are good yins, ma'am,' Donal said quietly. 'There's a maze.' He nodded towards the front door. 'It's newly planted so a body doesna' get lost, but ye can see the pattern.'

Melissa saw his wish to distract her, and as she had nothing else to do, decided to humour him. 'Thank you, Donal. Some air would be good for me. Do I turn left or right?'

'In the maze, ma'am? Oh, ye mean oot the door. Go tae the right and walk doon the path under them limes. It's flat.'

'Thank you, Donal. Could someone send Joanie to me, please? I would do better with a shawl.'

She followed Donal's instructions and wished he'd been less enthusiastic about the path being flat. Tree roots abounded, but she moved slowly — how else? — and soon the maze came into view. The bushes were as high as her thighs. She could stand on a raised mound prepared for the purpose to study the outline. It was peaceful.

She watched Joanie step out briskly along the path and after a moment, the colonel. What did he want now? His longer stride caught Joanie by surprise, and he relieved her of the shawl she was carrying before he sent her back to the house.

'I am not allowed the ordering of even my own servants,' she said when the big man came to stand beside her. She stood while he wrapped the shawl around her shoulders and was glad of its warmth. Shivers wracked her frame, and she knew the shock was still there waiting to ambush her and bring hot tears.

'I wanted a moment or two of privacy, and she is within calling distance. I have not isolated you, ma'am.' Harry Gunn lifted a large hand and ran his fingers through the blond hair once more.

'I trust you have not come to promote any liaisons with members of your family.' Melissa stared unseeingly over the maze. 'I cannot emphasise strongly enough how distasteful I find your sister's assertions.'

'That does not surprise me, ma'am. Many find her conclusions lack the benefit of rounded consideration.' He stopped teasing his hair and gripping her chin with one hand brought her face round. Melissa did not struggle, although her first instinct was to shield the scars down her right side.

'I think your right eye is less inflamed this morning. Do you have blurring when you are able to look through it?'

'Not now, no. The sight is clear enough, it is only that the eyelid droops.' She realised how clearly she'd seen Donal in the corridor where the light was muted. Maybe there was less of a problem this morning. The colonel grunted.

'That's the kind of noise Zed makes when he has to listen to me or Joanie,' she said, and the reflection brought a smile to her face.

'Beg pardon, ma'am. I think we need to apply one of our salves to the skin around that eye. It is dried out and stretched.' He let go her chin and she missed the warmth of his fingers. 'I have tried to tell you why I have removed you from your home, but there have been so many interruptions.'

'Yes.'

'My distant cousin, George Gunn, is the son of a father who ended his days in a bedlam,' Harry said, and she thought it sounded as if he drew the words from a well of misery.

'I am sorry to learn that, but it does not influence my decision. It is George himself I wish to have nothing to do with.' *And how I wish it were less than nothing. The man is morbid.*

'It does, however, influence my decision to bring you away . . . '

'Abduct.'

'Please, ma'am, I find this hard, and I would explain.' He straightened, and she saw again how very powerful he was. The material of his country clothing strained as his shoulders went back, and fire flashed in the depth of his wonderful eyes. Melissa drew breath. Not since Neville's early death had she felt the kind of stirrings she was experiencing in the colonel's company.

'My Great Uncle John is of an even older generation than George's papa, who was also called George. He remembers how that man's behaviour became at first an embarrassment and then bordered on the criminal. He pursued a liaison with a young woman, a girl really, just into her third Season and newly betrothed.'

Melissa began to understand what Harry Gunn was telling her, and she chilled. The younger George was doing the same over her.

'Surely your cousin simply wants to marry me and rob me?' she protested, but already she began to see that it might not be simple. It might not be about her wealth at all.

'Would that that was all. I am sure you have lawyers in plenty to deal with fortune hunters. Although many women do fall prey to practised seducers, you have the air of good sense that makes me believe you are not one of them.'

'And I am no longer seventeen. My family were not best pleased that Neville was my first and very early choice,' she replied, and watched Gunn's skin flare as the truth hit home. Some of her family could only now bring themselves to correspond with her, although some had rallied to her help after Neville died, and yet others after the fire. She was not alone, but they had not understood her fears over George Gunn. It seemed as if the colonel did.

'You are telling me you have been flighty once,' Gunn asked.

'Flighty?' She tested the word. 'I have never been flighty, sir. In fact, I was serious and well educated beyond most of my friends and hopefuls in my

Season. It was what attracted Neville to me, he said.'

'He admired your intellect, ma'am? When your beauty was legendary?' The colonel was teasing, if his tone told her anything. She responded in the same vein.

'And I was in possession of a very considerable fortune. The makings of marriage are mysterious, are they not? So few husbands allow their wives a voice, and yet Neville did.' Melissa shivered again. She resisted the temptation to look around her to check whether George was lurking in the dappled shade.

'It is cool here under the trees. We should walk back to the house perhaps.' Gunn clearly thought he'd explained everything she needed to know, and Melissa felt a flash of irritation. They had been getting on better, but he wanted to give her as little information as he could get away with after all.

'Why you, sir? Why not write to my London solicitors?'

'We did write to a Mr Withershaws in Newcastle. At least, my uncle did. He received a letter in reply that might be at best described as patronising of my uncle's advanced years, and at worst malicious.' Harry spoke with evident reluctance.

'Mr Withershaws is one of my principle concerns. There is a streak of malice in his nature, I agree.' Melissa wondered briefly about the wisdom of discussing her business affairs with Harry Gunn when she had known him such a short time. On the other hand, he was equally unhappy about Withershaws, which inspired some confidence.

'Has he made your life unpleasant since the earl died?'

'Oh yes,' Melissa agreed. 'Just as he made it very, very unpleasant when I married and my affairs passed into the hands of the earl's lawyers.' She reflected on those months of wrangling while she and Neville set up home and he tried to understand the complexities of owning and operating manufactories.

He had not been bred to business as she had, and they were difficult times as well as being months of delirious romance.

'Withershaws said among his legal cronies that Neville contaminated the bloodline by marrying into trade. At the same time, he has told me more than once how well I played my cards.' Melissa hoped the condensing of all that the man had said and done into such a bald statement would not damn her soul in time, but she could not reveal all of Withershaw's malignant behaviour to a comparative stranger.

'Ah.' Gunn offered his arm and Melissa took it. 'Then Mr Withershaws believes all commoners are in want of a title?'

'It would seem he does, sir. He had not long been my papa's lawyer, of course.' Melissa felt the familiar wave of irritation she experienced when thoughts of Withershaws's obstructions filled her head. 'He would not have been kept on by *him*, but my uncles have been a little too trusting. Despite his strongest efforts, I have kept my affairs out of his hands, and retain the services of Battle and Wharton of Lincoln's Inn.' Melissa moved slowly beside the colonel. The pace allowed her to think over her many grievances with Mr Withershaws. She had been so close to relieving him of her uncles' business before the fire.

'I suppose, ma'am, there's no doubt over the cause of the fire that destroyed the London house?' Colonel Gunn sounded hopeful, and she hated to disappoint him, but facts were facts.

'There had been a build-up of thundery weather over several days. At the end of June, it broke, and the household went to bed happier. Cook would not have the milk turned. The air would be fresher.' She paused, but the colonel did not add any remarks about weather, so she carried on with her tale. 'Around nine in the evening, the storm came overhead. There was an explosion as the house was struck, and within minutes we were on fire. The floor of my room gave way, and I fell on my mattress through two stories until everything landed in the kitchen. I was trapped by a roof beam and unconscious.'

'Mercifully,' he said, and she heard the gentleness there. Turning to view his beautiful face, she surprised a look she had seen before on the face of one other. It was what she had fallen in love with in Neville's face — unadorned admiration.

★   ★   ★

Harry's breath left him with the speed it did when an opponent landed one in his solar plexus. He was momentarily confounded.

The intelligent grey eyes studying him from Melissa's damaged face were full of recognition. Did the girl see, albeit in and out of focus, how she was affecting him? He distanced himself and caused her to stumble forward in small steps while she regained her balance.

'My lady, I am sorry.' He mumbled the words and caught her arm by the elbow to steady her. She was so thin, it further wrenched his heart, and he fought for air. What was happening?

'Colonel, you are very red of a sudden. Are you unwell?' Harry pulled himself together. What purpose would be served by adding to the lady's anxieties?

'No, ma'am, not unwell. No, I never feel better than when I am in the country with my men and the weather is set fair. All I lack for perfection are my bitches.' *Now I'm prosing on and making very little sense*, he thought. His head was light, and years of uncertainty fell away as if they'd been a cloak tied by an invisible thread. He was in love.

I am capable of love.

Harry checked his stride. Melissa Pateley walked slowly and took care while placing her feet. She had made a good recovery from desperate injury, but she had a lot of healing still to do. Harry was surrounded by recovering soldiers and gave medical advice to many agricultural workers, and their families when they could be persuaded to consult with him. He was able to make an estimate of their chances in most cases.

It looks to me, he thought, *as if it will take Lady Pateley another three months of careful exercise and equally careful diet before she is anywhere near as fit as she was before the fire. Her skin will never be restored.* Realising he was in danger of giving himself away, Harry sought a different topic. 'How do your relations with the new earl do?' he asked.

'Charles Pateley is a small grey man in his seventies. His wife died many years ago, but unlike me, she did present her lord with an heir before that sad event.' Melissa spoke without rancour. 'He is not antipathetic to me, and indeed I stayed on in Neville's battered townhouse with his blessing.'

'So there are few irritations in your relations with the estate . . . '

'Very few; and such as they are, they lie entirely at the hand of Mr Withershaws.' Melissa stopped and turned towards him. He looked down into female eyes cloudy with emotion. 'At first, he pretended nothing could be done until it was clear whether I was carrying a male heir or not.' She hesitated, as if considering how he might receive such a frank statement.

'Surely that is reasonable, ma'am? It would be unkind to install a Charles to the earldom if he was to be usurped within a year.' Harry was all reason-ableness, hoping she would not be overcome by embarrassment.

'Of course, but Mr Withershaws persisted for eighteen months.' She shuddered.

'The memories of that time must be hard to live with, even now.'

'When it became clear that I was not to be blessed with Neville's child,

Withershaws' efforts to gain control of my assets intensified. Can you imagine, sir, the man wrote as if on behalf of my uncles? He took it upon himself to arrange a meeting with the partners of Battle and Wharton.' Melissa drew a steadying breath. 'Only after my uncles agreed to hear me speak did his position become less certain.'

'I can readily understand how much frustration all of this has added to your grief over Lord Pateley's death.' Harry did understand why Melissa was so concerned. The late Sir Richard Flaxxe had been a man of huge wealth. He had industrial properties in Newcastle, Glasgow and Manchester. He was also a renowned collector of paintings and the owner of two country estates and several townhouses, as well as the rows and rows of small houses built for his mill workers. It was not by any means unusual for relatives to consider a woman, no matter her capabilities and strengths, unequal to the task of running them. Several ladies had found themselves incarcerated in institutions by the men of their families in such circumstances.

'Withershaws might not be the best man to further the businesses,' Melissa said quietly. 'My late husband was not very gifted in business matters either. I always talked things through with him before he attended meetings,' she said. Harry saw the concern pucker her brow. 'It is now nearly three years since I and the men of the Flaxxe and Baxter families took control of our works and work-forces. I have been unable to shake Withershaws from my uncles' affairs, as the elder suffered a seizure, and it is not possible to learn what his instructions are. The younger men keep the infernal man on in order to see what he instructs and advises.' She ran a hand down the length of her skirt and raised her chin. 'I am sadly awaiting my uncle's death and his eldest son's succession in order to oust the lawyer.'

'Withershaws in charge might be like a regiment being commanded by an admiral,' Harry mused, and was delighted with the small answering laugh. He thought that aside from the matter of the fire, it might have been a long time since Melissa Pateley had things to laugh over.

'Much worse, sir. More like a warship being commanded by a general of foot.'

★ ★ ★

Melissa was tired by her walk to the maze, but the time spent in Harry Gunn's company had restored her good humour and raised her spirits. She began to think that with a man like him as her ally, she would soon rout Withershaws. Although her own lawyers had control of the family fortunes, it was constantly wearisome to have to argue every decision against the man's contrariness. Many of her relatives relied on their connection with the various mills and estates to survive. There were also a certain number of pensioners, and she knew Withershaws had been making life very hard for some of them by refusing to honour the agreements her papa had set in place.

And all the while, of course, I must remember never to be trapped alone with him. What would Harry Gunn say if I told him of Withershaws's plan to impregnate me once it became clear I was not pregnant with Neville's heir?

'My lady,' Joanie said as she came into the entrance hall. The colonel had gone round to the stables with a murmured excuse about seeing to his horse.

'Joanie, I am glad you returned to the house. The biting insects are quite bad below the trees.' She saw one or two red blotches lifting on her maid's chin. 'You've been bitten.'

'I have, my lady. That Zed person says he'll give me a preparation to help with the itch.' Joanie lifted a hand to scratch and then stopped. 'I might break the skin, but oh, it does itch.'

Melissa smiled. She certainly knew well how that felt. 'Were you going to give me some news?'

'Yes, my lady, sorry. Zed has asked me to tell you he'll wait on you in your room in twenty minutes,' Joanie said, and dipped her gaze. Melissa looked at the blush covering the girl's neck. It was something for a soldier to tell a countess he would wait on her. And also for her loyal staff to let him think he might.

'Wait on me?' she said. 'Why would Zed wait on me?'

'It's the exercises, my lady.' Clearly Joanie thought this was sufficient explanation, but when Melissa did not move towards the staircase, she was forced to expand. 'For your right arm. There are exercises that will bring it back almost to what it was, but he has to show us first.'

Melissa heard the throb of excitement in Joanie's voice. The girl was caught up by the prospect of help for her injuries, but she wondered whether she could permit this man to attend her. Lottie Duart was loud in her condemnation, maybe too loud, but she did have a point. Why did these unschooled soldiers think they knew anything about the injuries of civilians?

'Lady Pateley,' Zed spoke from very close. 'I'm sorry to startle you, my lady. I was explaining to this young person that the colonel and I had decided how best to manipulate your arm.' Zed moved towards the stairs, and Melissa watched him closely. He was, like his master the colonel, used to command. The rough features hardly unbent as he studied her from deep-set eyes.

He expects me to follow him without argument.

'You are carrying a milking stool,' she said.

'He will sit at your feet, ma'am. Like one of the mortals in the court of the Goddess.' Harry Gunn must have decided to leave his horses in peace and disturb her instead, because he spoke from the shadows. Melissa cast him a withering glance over her shoulder.

'It's all very well for you to make a

joke, sir, but you must see how very unorthodox all this is.' She knew it was pettish, but Melissa had a feeling the manipulation Zed talked of would be anything other than benign.

'Hmn! Do I detect a trace of nervousness? Zed comes to you as a skilled practitioner, no matter what canker my sister may have set in your brain.'

Melissa quailed. Gunn had taken very little effort to work out what truly troubled her about the prospect.

'Perhaps you would be present, sir,' Zed said, and she heard Harry's sharp intake of breath. They all recognised the challenge from his second in command. Harry had all but admitted the previous evening that Zed had a stronger stomach for the cases needing surgery. Would he also find it too hard to be present if his man reduced her to tears? She straightened her shoulders as far as her damaged muscles allowed.

'There is no need for that. Joanie will be sufficient escort.' She wondered if it were true. Would Joanie be able to catch her if Zed's ministrations caused her to swoon?

'Nonsense. Zed refines too much on one or two incidents when I'd been up for days on end and had no food. Your maid may not be able to prevent a fall if . . . if a fall should happen.' Harry sounded less sure of this coming procedure than she was herself, but Zed brimmed with confidence.

'If you would be good enough to sit on this chair, my lady?' Zed asked once they'd all assembled in Melissa's chamber. She watched him position the three-legged stool and seat himself at her side.

Harry Gunn crossed to the windows and gazed out over the policies. His broad shoulders blocked the light, and Zed glanced his way. She was momentarily distracted by the ripple of muscle beneath the colonel's coat, and when she turned back to Zed, caught a stiffening in that man's body. His eyes flashed, but when he realised she was watching him and his colonel, he quickly hooded them.

'Colonel, I think you are blocking the light by standing there,' Melissa said. It was a few seconds before Gunn responded, and she began to shiver. 'What is it out there that holds your attention so closely?'

'Nothing, ma'am. You are, however, correct to point out that I'm blocking the light, and I will leave Zed to his ministrations.'

She did not miss the glance that was exchanged between the men as the colonel strode from the room. Whatever he had seen in the policies was clearly in need of urgent attention.

I suspect George has worked his way back onto the estate.

'Ogilvie!' The door crashed shut on Gunn's call to one of the men. Zed spoke quickly, and the question she was forming slid from her mind for the moment.

'Now, my lady, the exercises I am going to show you and Joanie are not intended to hurt at all. What I find works most is when the patient does them every day, two or three times in the day.' Zed's hands pushed up the cloth of her sleeve and gripped her right arm. This morning she was well enough to notice his skin was not rough or calloused, but smooth and warm. That surprised Melissa, although she wasn't sure why it should.

'Two or three times,' she said faintly. How long were her injuries going to occupy so much of every waking hour?

'Please try to grip my hand.'

For half an hour Melissa did as Zed instructed, and Joanie watched closely. She began to feel tired, and knew she would slip into a doze if allowed to lie on the bed.

'You are tired for today, my lady,' Zed said. He drew her sleeve down and stood up. 'If Joanie would help you repeat these stretches this afternoon before the meal, I would be pleased.'

'You are a hard task master,' Melissa said as she watched the man lift his stool. 'Tell me, why did the colonel depart so suddenly?'

Zed stopped on his way to the door and turned back so she could see the side of his face. A grudging smile was lingering there.

'He had hoped for some shooting in Colonel Paxton's absence. Only pigeon of course. Game is little sought until September.'

'Pigeon,' she mused. 'I formed the impression he was studying something larger beneath the tree line, not in the tops.' Melissa shrugged. Zed was not going to give away anything his master might not want her to learn. It was pointless to tease him.

'Some sleep would benefit your ladyship.' Zed made his final laconic observation before bowing and leaving them.

'I think you're in the right of it, my lady,' Joanie said as soon as the bedroom door closed on Melissa's strange physician. 'The colonel clenched them fists of his all right and tight, he did. And then he was off shouting at the men. I ain't heard him shout.'

Nor have I, Melissa thought. Whatever caught his eye below the trees, it wasn't a flight of pigeon.

6

Melissa sank into a sleep tormented by dreams. George Gunn sat in her papa's chair at one end of a long table and watched silently while her relatives squabbled among themselves. His chiselled countenance hardly moved, and Melissa's exhausted brain teased itself further. Pointless questions swam in her head. How many muscles would a man need to hold in check if he were intent on keeping his expression and thoughts hidden?

Lottie Duart appeared from nowhere. She stood behind George's shoulder and laid a small hand on it.

'Come now, Lady Pateley. The only way to defeat this charlatan Withershaws is by taking a forceful and intelligent husband. We women do not need to tease our smaller brains with the workings of mills and mines.' The vision smiled and Melissa's heart constricted.

Even in sleep, she wondered why it concerned Mrs Duart so much. Why did she set her opinion against her brother's while telling Melissa to give up her power of thought to a man?

Eventually, Melissa let the struggle go and opened her eyes. The right one responded more quickly than it had even yesterday, and her sight adjusted to the light. Since Joanie had drawn the curtains, the room was dim, and it was a few seconds before she was sure of what she was looking at.

He sat in the chair by the fireside. Large and still, his legs stretched at ease across the hearth rugs. One booted foot rested on the other. Melissa stifled a scream, but her heart thumped. Where were Harry and Zed and even the man Ogilvie, whose face she could not bring to mind? Why was George Gunn so capable of sliding like a serpent past guards and servants alike?

'You are awake, my dear,' he said;

and the measured vowels brought cold shivers to Melissa's undamaged skin and a tingling sensation across her scalp. 'That idiot colonel and his band of damaged heroes are chasing around the grounds. Without dogs, they are hampered.'

Melissa lay silent. George Gunn had not attacked her or even touched her very often in the past when he'd forced his way into her houses, but she could not be certain he was never going to do so. She could not know when his disordered view of the world would tempt him to believe it was organised as he thought.

'He said I should not expect you to answer me, Melissa, but there will come a time when your froideur melts. Neville Pateley is dead; and a woman such as you, intelligent and passionate, must long to know the comfort of a kindred heart.' He turned then and eased himself off the chair.

Melissa heard the outer doors clattering downstairs, but her tongue was tied in fright. She did not call out or scream because she could not. George's persistence brought about a paralysis in her she did not understand. Had he turned the key? The lock was modern, and no doubt Mrs Paxton kept it well oiled. She watched him pace across the room until he stood over her.

'This cat-and-mouse game is exhausting, my dear,' he said as if addressing a schoolroom chit who spent her days flirting with visiting cousins. 'I will have you.' He leaned over the bed, and she shrank from the overexcited gleam in his eyes. 'I will. And believe me, my dear Melissa, if I cannot have you, then no other man will.' His fingers traced a path down the damaged skin of her right cheek and gripped her chin.

Melissa screamed.

★   ★   ★

Harry stood aside as Zed, Percy and Matt rushed the countess's room and crossed to the gaping window. George must have dropped out of it, and the men gazed down. Harry knew there was a tiny balcony above the saloon. From there, George had most likely clambered hand over hand down an established ivy that covered the walls. Zed would not be able to get him in his sights because of the thick growth. They all knew it would be useless to discharge pistols across the distance between them and their quarry when he came back into view.

'I did wonder whether that ivy was a temptation, but the man is as tall as I, and I disregarded it. I am very sorry, your ladyship.' Harry stood watching the men shake their heads and their fists in despair. One by one they left the room, and Joanie came in to replace them. Harry sent Melissa a glance he knew was full of anguish. This could have been a disaster.

'He is very clever, colonel,' Melissa said. He watched the struggle reflected in her eyes. Was she blaming him and his men for their abject failure? They deserved no less.

'We are the trained soldiers. He makes us look like trained monkeys.' Behind him, Joanie giggled nervously. 'He has achieved this before?'

'Oh yes. Twice in London. Then three weeks ago, he was already in the Pateley hunting lodge at Ludlow when we arrived . . . '

He saw Melissa draw breath. It was deep, and she swallowed hard before continuing. 'On these occasions, I rang for Percy and Matt, and it caused him to make a ridiculous bow and leave. Tonight — ' She stopped and Harry felt the hairs on the back of his neck stand away from his skin. 'Tonight he came and leaned over the bed. He said if he could not have me, then no one would.'

Joanie let out a squeal of fright. 'My lady, the beast is in him. He is the devil.' The girl began to sob, and Harry turned to her.

'Joanie, this will not help your mistress. Please go to my cook and ask him to fortify you with some of his brandy.' Without waiting for either mistress or maid to react, he gripped the girl by the shoulders and pitched her onto the landing. It wasn't possible to lock the door because they'd had to blast their way in, and the fixture hung by a few shreds of splintered wood.

'We will have to reinstate Mrs Paxton's woodwork,' Melissa said. She sounded calmer, and he turned back to her.

'My lady, I am truly more sorry than I can express.'

'Then do not say anything else, Colonel. You rescued me, and perhaps now we may agree about how very mad your cousin is.'

'I never truly doubted Uncle John, ma'am; but as you say, George is a serious case.'

'Indeed. Until today, I thought he wanted the money alone. I have been wrong. I have been very, very wrong,' she said; but anything else she would have added was caught by a sob.

Harry bowed deeply and left. He was not surprised to find Joanie hovering on the landing. He let her pass into the room so she could help Melissa to rise from her afternoon rest.

He dropped to the next landing, but catching sight of Zed pacing in the ground floor hall, he continued down. The man was agitated, and Harry suspected he knew why.

'You want to move on, Zed. You think we would be better protected in George Square with so many friends around us.'

'Aye, well, maister, we might be, but I'm dumb-foonered by that man's audacity.' Zed clenched a fist around the handle of the silver dagger he normally wore strapped to his calf. Harry studied him in silence. It wasn't usual for Zed to lapse into local speech when they were alone. George was affecting them all, and not for the better.

'I understand that, and would have agreed with you until my sister made her observations this morning. I am wondering why she is so very keen to promote an alliance.'

'What alliance?' Zed asked sharply.

'Why, she sees our work with the men as depleting the Gunn estate and believes George's marriage to the countess would help the coffers recover.' Harry drew the words from a depth. Despite their closeness over more than a decade, he did not normally discuss the family with his sergeant.

'She cannot for one moment think George Gunn has any intention of assisting the family in general,' Zed said, and Harry knew he was puzzled, too. 'The accounts for our small factories are beginning to turn from loss to profit. With the continuing peace, folk are more ready to buy luxury goods like soap. It was a good product to produce.'

'I know. She would know, if she was interested.' He resented the constant carping criticism Lottie directed his way. It infected family relations whenever the subject of his medical work came up in conversation.

'Maybe Mistress Duart has something else on her mind, sir.'

Harry cast Zed a quizzical look, but the sergeant was a picture of serenity. He wondered. what would prompt a normally sensible woman to suggest the idiocy of a match between Lady Pateley and George Gunn.

★　★　★

Melissa entered the dining room and was pleased to see Harry Gunn ahead of her. He had changed his linen and his man had shaved him, enhancing the structure of his bones until his beauty was all but painful for her to look at. She must have imagined the admiration she saw in his eyes earlier, she thought. No man who looked like the colonel need trouble himself over the ruination that was her appearance.

'Good afternoon, ma'am,' he said,

and Melissa's heart sank further. Such politeness did not augur well. 'Zed and I have been considering the options open to us, and if your ladyship is agreeable, we will rise early and depart for Edinburgh.'

'Can the journey be completed in one day?' She accepted the chair Harry held for her in front of the open fireplace. 'I have not been making such long stages in my own journey north from London.'

'You have the right of it, ma'am, it would be too long for both the horses and yourself. It is our wish to help you recover, not to cause any sort of relapse.' Harry stood in front of the fireplace as if it had coals to warm his breeches, and Melissa suppressed a smile when he lifted his coat tails to do just that. He dropped them with a small flurry of embarrassment. 'There are friends in Haddington whose house is large enough to accommodate us and whose grounds will allow the men to camp.'

'Simmerton?'

'No, one would not wish to subject him to that again. I am sure there will be a suitable indoor bed for all three of your men servants.' Silence developed.

Harry moved about and seemed relieved when the door opened and the butler appeared carrying a tray with decanters. Percy followed, bringing another with glasses and a dish or two of almond biscuits. Melissa asked her men one or two questions, and when she was satisfied that they were being occupied and fed, let them go.

'You are a little agitated, Colonel. Will you not sit down and tell me about Edinburgh? I have never been there, and while this visit comes as a surprise, I wonder what you think I ought to see.' She tried not to accuse him again, but her words did bring his head up abruptly, and a flash of something like anger lit his wonderful hazel eyes. She tried not to liken him to an avenging Greek god and failed. Harry Gunn was an extraordinary man.

'I cannot go on apologising for my actions.' He refilled his glass from the brandy decanter and sat down in a chair with arms. 'We have agreed that George Gunn is a dangerous and probably deranged individual.'

'We have; and I do not quarrel with you, sir, but there are innumerable difficult questions resulting from your actions. Will there be enough space for me and my people in your Edinburgh house, for example?' Melissa hoped her desperation did not imbue her words. She was much shaken by George's threat, and now found she wanted to be surrounded by men who had her best interests at heart.

'No'

'No?'

'The house in George Square will not accommodate all of us, as my sisters are all visiting Mama at present. However, my uncle's house is a mere hundred yards away in Charles Street. I will suggest to my sisters that they move into his establishment while you are our guest.' She saw the look that suffused his features. It had the effect of both longing and despair mingled and competing. Tremors of excitement shook her. Even the possibility that Harry Gunn might see her as a woman and not simply an encumbrance of his honour was exciting.

'So your mama continues to live in your house?' Melissa knew Edinburgh was a city dominated by its ministers and that the Scottish kirk was a powerful institution. She could not afford to live in Harry's house without a proper chaperone or her reputation would be tainted. Given the energy George Gunn was putting into destroying her name already, she thought it would be best to ensure she did nothing herself to add fuel to his fire.

'For much of the year.' Harry frowned, and the gravitas made him look exactly like the commander he must have been in the field. 'My mama now finds the rigours of our country estate more than she wishes to deal with in winter.' He emptied his glass and set it down with a decided thump.

Melissa blinked. What had brought that edge of steel to the colonel's words? She risked another glance into his face and blinked again. What had Mrs Gunn done to cause such turmoil in her only son?

7

Too soon, dinner drew to a close. Harry Gunn had been an entertaining host and attentive to her injuries. Small attentions, such as having the cook-man make a stew of meat with vegetables instead of a roast, enabled her to eat without asking that someone should cut it up. She began to smile more freely at little things.

'Lady Pateley, in Zed's absence, I will not be attending your scars this evening. I will give Joanie the fresh batch of salve and ensure her hands are as clean as they may be. I hope she will not recoil from the application she must use.' Harry Gunn spoke quietly without taking his eyes from her face, and Melissa was aware of every dried and overlaid wrinkle of skin down the right side. Heat suffused her left side, but the colonel did not drop his gaze to allow her to recover her composure.

'I realised Zed was not eating with us, but I did not know what your habits might be,' she said.

'He has gone ahead to Edinburgh to make arrangements for our arrival. If you are asking whether we normally eat together, then that depends on the company.' The colonel was tense now, she thought. Because it was of importance to him, she asked about the application he expected Joanie to use.

'It will dye her hands.'

'Purpley-brown. You and Zed both have staining on your hands. Will it wear off? Joanie has been my most loyal helper, but she is young, and the young — '

'The young have their vanity. I am needed to supervise the men in Zed's absence, but I am loath to let a day go past when you do not have the application. I will impress this on her.' He stood up then and came behind her chair.

'Thank you, Colonel, for all of your

help. I do realise the oddness of my circumstances in relation to George Gunn, but I will write to my aunt Flaxxe and my cousins, from Edinburgh.' She felt the warmth of his fingers encircle her left arm and assist her to stand. He drew the chair away, and for a few seconds she was dependent on his strength alone to support her. *It's as well he is such a strong man*, she thought, *although his very closeness makes me shakier than ever.*

'Are you steady, ma'am?'

'Yes, thank you. I think where Joanie is concerned, the promise of something to wash out the colour would be more effective than any stick.'

'I have younger sisters. Fortunately they have both married, and I am no longer reduced to apoplexy on a daily basis.' Harry stood away a little, and Melissa forced herself to move out from the table. 'But I remember well how one must approach these things.'

'You are unkind, I think. I am sure

that as your sisters are made of the same stuff as Mrs Duart, they will be sensible matrons.' Melissa could no longer bring herself to use Mrs Duart's given name.

'I will ask you whether your opinion is unchanged after you have enjoyed their conversation.' Harry's remark was tinged by an ironic laugh; and Melissa thought her stay among his relatives, although she would try to make it as short as possible, might be entertaining.

* * *

Harry escorted the countess up the two flights of stairs to her chamber, but did not enter it with her. He saw that the bath sat ready on the hearth rug and that one of his men had effected a repair to the lock. The young footman from the countess's staff sat on a padded stool to one side of the door with a strong cudgel across his knees.

'Is this necessary, sir?' Lady Pateley asked. 'Surely he has gone this time.'

'You are the one who saw the madness in his eyes, ma'am. Do you want to take the risk?' He saw the flash of near panic light her left eye and cursed himself for an insensitive fool. 'I know you are probably in the right of it, ma'am, but humour the soldiering instinct in me, please.'

'Of course. I suppose that like a buzzing insect, he will not be easily deterred.' Although she compared George to an insect, he reminded Harry more clearly of a snake, slithering and silent. No need to let the lady know that either.

'Exactly. I will seek out Joanie and see to the antiseptic.'

He descended to the kitchens, where Joanie was waiting for word, and sat down facing the girl. She flushed. Harry knew his looks had this kind of effect on women. All women of marriageable age, and many a bit older, melted in his gaze. However, he also knew that few young girls in Joanie's position had any real idea they would grace his bed. With nothing to gain by humouring him, she would be resistant to his suggestion about the antiseptic. He kept his expression serious.

'Your lady has healed well, Miss Joanie. Zed and I believe she would not have done nearly so well if only the expensive London doctors had been responsible for her care.' He saw the muscles in the girl's neck clench. He had her whole attention.

'Her ladyship is pleased with their work, sir,' she said mildly enough.

'As am I, but they diagnosed and prescribed. Where her treatment has triumphed has been in your unflinching assistance. I wonder whether you will consider using the same precautions as Zed and I have developed over many years treating battlefield wounds?'

'You think to make my hands all stained that purple and brown, like yourn?'

'Touché, Miss Joanie, I do.' Harry sat back. There was a justice to his comeuppance, he knew. Lady Pateley was never going to have employed a flighty piece, even if she'd demurred over his suggestion.

'I been talking with some of the men. They tell me how your patients don't get that hot fever that carries off so many even after their bleeding stops.'

Hot fever was a good description, and Harry nodded. 'We carry the ingredients around and make our own preparation.'

'I'll do it, sir. I want her ladyship to get better. I know you can't make her skin all smooth again, but . . . ' The girl trailed off, and Harry wondered if she hoped he would contradict her.

'I cannot perform miracles, Miss Joanie.' It was bleak, but also true.

After the girl went off to her mistress, Harry went into the Paxtons' saloon. He lit one or two candles and sat by the window with a book open on his lap. He had lied a little to Lady Pateley. The men did not need his supervision so soon into Zed's absence, but he needed to avoid her bedroom tonight.

He'd seen her naked, and held her close wrapped only in towels and when she was in her night things. Initially she had been a patient, interesting and in need of his attentions. How quickly that had changed, however; and he could no longer trust himself alone with her. She was not insensitive to him, he thought, but she was vulnerable and he would not take advantage.

The book slipped from his lap and hit the floor with a thump. There were other thoughts swimming in his brain, too. Why did Lottie seem intent on marrying off the injured stranger when it was no business of hers? He knew from bitter experience the influence she had and the damage she could wreak over the family.

Colonel Harry Gunn strode out into the night. He'd faced canon-fire and worse, but none of it had caused the gut-wrenching pain he now suffered.

★ ★ ★

Melissa sat in the window space and gazed onto the side garden where the shadows were deepening. It was neither late nor dark, but on this side of the modern house, the trees cast long shadows. Harry Gunn appeared from somewhere beneath her, walking briskly towards them.

'Is that the colonel, my lady?' Joanie asked. She'd stepped aside while the footmen emptied the bathwater and carried it out. Now she was teasing the locks of Melissa's wig and standing close to the window to catch as much light as possible.

'Yes; he's taller than all the other men. It must be him.' Melissa knew, but added the rider so Joanie would not think she could spot the colonel in the half-dark. She was surprising herself with her interest in him.

'He's an unusual man for to have been a soldier,' Joanie said. 'They all love him like their own fathers. I don't think there's one of them wouldn't die for him.'

'Goodness. Is that likely to be necessary?' Melissa asked mischievously.

'You may know what I mean, your ladyship, when I say as how they all live together and work together and don't go back to their townships, which is what they call a village. They make soap.' Joanie finished brushing and stood while Melissa thought over the information.

'Soap?'

'Yes, your ladyship. They have lots of little workshops, and they make it with different smells.' The girl set down the wig and dug into the pocket of her cotton gown. 'Donal gave me this.'

Melissa smelled the soap within seconds. It was mildly antiseptic, she thought, and she could see it was not a pristine new piece. 'That's an interesting smell, Joanie.' She inhaled again, but wasn't able to identify the scent.

'I think it's myrtle, my lady. The men say it keeps them pesky little biting flies away.' Joanie dropped it back into her pocket and lifted the wig again.

'Midges,' Melissa whispered. How she wished there was something similar she could use to get rid of George Gunn.

8

Melissa strained to see the front of the terrace of houses in George Square when their carriages pulled up there three days later. A light rain was falling, but the air was fresh and the clouds were high above, scudding in front of a strong breeze. Harry was at the foot of the steps to assist her from the vehicle.

'I hope your hat ribbons are securely tied, ma'am. The Edinburgh wind steals anything not fastened down.' He held her arm below the elbow and took her weight as she negotiated the steps.

'I think I am able to make the descent more easily than even four days ago, Colonel.' The wind did snatch at her skirts, but there was a joyous feel to its impertinence. Melissa chided herself silently for such a fanciful thought. Where had it come from?

'Lady Pateley,' Zed spoke from the

pavement flags, and was soon across to make a bow and steady Joanie as the maid tripped off the carriage steps. 'Colonel, Mistress Gunn awaits you and your visitor in the upstairs drawing room. Mistress Duart is with her.'

Harry's hand tensed on her arm and Melissa suppressed a squeal of discomfort. Which of the ladies caused him the greater degree of anxiety, his mama or his sister?

'Perhaps you wish to see your ladies alone in the first instance, sir?'

'And perhaps I do not, ma'am.'

Harry's hand relaxed a little, and they set off towards the front steps of his townhouse with its platt leading to a wide door.

'That is an arresting shade of red,' she said involuntarily; and then, lest Harry should think she was criticising his mother's taste, added, 'But most attractive and cheerful.'

'Yes,' he said, and she knew he was mulling over something. They had lapsed into an easy way of conversation over the days since Zed left them and George had been ejected. He had not dismissed her remarks as if she were a wife of long standing.

That brought Melissa to a halt, and she felt Harry stumble a little at her side. A wife? Did she want to be anyone's wife again? Did she want to be Harry Gunn's wife?

'Are you quite well, ma'am?' Harry did sound as if he wanted to know whether she was or not. He infused warmth and interest into his tone and his words.

'Yes, quite. A momentary hesitation is all.' She wondered if her expression held any clue of the turmoil roiling inside her. She'd known she might want to marry again, having been widowed so young, but the fire had pushed it out of mind. Besides the attentions of men who thought she was on her deathbed and therefore a source of funds, and George Gunn in his particular madness, she had had from that point no notion that any man would want her again. Suddenly it seemed a little possible that Harry might, and moreover that she might want him back. It was a thrilling discovery.

'We keep the drawing room on the first floor. Will you allow me to assist you on the stairs? They follow the sweep of the wall and become a little narrow out from the corners.'

'Thank you, sir,' Melissa replied. Although she felt her balance was much restored and her grip strengthening every day, a strange staircase might hold some surprises, and she had no wish to tumble down it.

Mrs Gunn rose to greet her visitors and accepted a warm embrace from her son. Melissa saw a tall angular woman of some age, but in robust health. She wore a fashionable gown in a deep violet shade which was embellished around the neckline by an edge of ivory lace.

'Good afternoon, Lady Pateley,' Mrs Gunn said, and extended a hand.

Melissa thought she would risk accepting it and was happy when the older woman did not grip her fingers too tightly. She brought her left hand up, too, and patted Melissa gently. It was as if she was showing her concern for the younger woman's plight and the loss of her beauty.

'My lady,' Mrs Gunn said in a flutter, 'I hope I have not hurt your hand?'

'No, ma'am, no you have not. I find my eyes water considerably in the aftermath of the fire, but they are so much better than they were.' She trotted the lie out with all the conviction she could manage, but even so Harry's eyebrows rose a little.

'Nae doubt Zed has been treating ye. He and Harry aye have some new potion or salve on the go.' Mrs Gunn sounded rather proud of her son, and his helpmeet and Melissa smiled.

'Mama, you should not encourage them. Indeed, you promised to have your personal physician call on Lady Pateley as soon as might be convenient.'

Lottie Duart evidently could wait no longer before advancing her belief that Harry and his sergeant were amusing themselves in civilian life with a little medical dalliance. Melissa felt the hairs on the left side of her nape lift and shiver. What was this woman trying to achieve with her constant carping?

'Good afternoon, Mrs Duart,' she said, and added firmly, 'I have no need of any further medical attention at present, thank you. Mrs Gunn, it was most kind of you to think of it, but I am feeling . . . ' Melissa straggled to a halt. What *was* she feeling? she wondered. 'Alive' was the word that popped up in her brain, but like considering the wind to be impertinent, it was too fanciful. 'I am feeling better than at any time since the fire. I know Zed's exercises are strengthening my arm and wrist, and the salve Harry has given me is helping my skin breathe once more.'

Out of the corner of her good eye, she saw a bright pink suffuse Harry's complexion. She accepted a seat close to Mrs Gunn on a sofa. The fire was laid in the grate, but not lit; and as the room faced west, the air remained warm.

Mrs Duart did not sit down, but paced a little across the rugs. Eventually her mama asked whether she intended to stay on for the meal or to go to her uncle's.

'I can see Harry's return has befuddled you, Mama, as it so often does. However, I will go to Uncle John's house. Kitty and Mairie have promised to come to you tomorrow.' She lifted a reticule from the seat of a chair and smiled. Melissa found little warmth in the smile and gazed back without responding. 'Will it be too much for your health, my lady, to meet my sisters tomorrow?'

'No, I look forward to meeting them. Colonel Gunn has spoken of them at some length.' Melissa hoped her reply was sufficiently welcoming. She did not intend to trespass on Mrs Gunn's hospitality for too long, so it would be good to meet the ladies as early as possible. Lottie nodded and left the room gracefully.

★   ★   ★

'My daughter is wont to become excitable,' Mrs Gunn said with a sideways glance at her son. They heard doors opening and servants moving on the stairs. 'She was out of the schoolroom before Harry's arrival meant she had a surviving sibling, and I do wonder whether her status as an only child for so long . . . ' The old lady brought her hand over her mouth, and Melissa watched in fascination as her eyes widened further than she thought anyone's eyes could.

'You worry that I will see comparisons, ma'am,' Melissa said mildly, 'because I never acquired that sibling. Alas, I know how much grief my behaviour left behind me and how well deserved any suggestion of wilfulness is. I was not easily guided, but I did love my husband; and despite all that has happened since, we were happy in the years we had together.'

Mrs Gunn sent her a grateful smile, but Harry's frown deepened to such an extent that Melissa thought he looked like a bloodhound. What had she said? Surely her effort was all in trying to ease her hostess's embarrassment, and so he should be pleased?

'Lady Pateley has commented on how similar George Gunn and I are, Mama. I find his colouring is much darker than mine,' Harry said slowly.

'Do you, my dear? George is not a very close cousin, and the females whose families dilute his Gunn bloodline are not the same as the ones in yours.' Mrs Gunn shifted on the seat beside her, and Melissa saw a sheen erupt across the lady's forehead. 'It has to be said that your papa was surprised by how very flaxen — '

'Mrs Gunn,' Melissa squealed as the lady slid down the seat. Harry caught her before she landed on the floor.

'Simmerton!' Seeing the colonel struggling with his mama's weight and the awkward position of her body, Melissa called out to her butler and then to Percy. The men came into the room. Percy set down one of Melissa's travelling cases and moved to help the colonel.

'Thank you, both.' Melissa stood up shakily and moved out of their way. She watched the men lower Mrs Gunn to the rugs, and with her stronger left hand, she straightened the lady's skirts around her ankles.

'Simmerton, would you ask Zed to come up, please?' Harry spoke softly, but she heard the anxiety in his voice and — something else: a sadness, perhaps.

'Is your mama wont to swoon?' she asked Harry, but kept her eyes fixed on Mrs Gunn's face. All the healthy colour had drained away and the lady looked every one of her years. Melissa remembered the fan she had tucked into her reticule and brought it out.

'Thank you, ma'am. If you would allow me to slide this under Mama's feet . . . ' Harry was fast regaining his business-like approach to illness, and Melissa moved aside again. He slipped a cushion below his mother's ankles and then allowed her to open the fan and cool the lady with it. By the time Zed appeared in the doorway, Mrs Gunn was opening her eyes and gazing around in a little confusion.

'Lie still, Mama,' Harry ordered quietly. Zed and Simmerton came into the room with a woman Melissa assumed was Mrs Gunn's maid. 'Lie still, please. Here's Janet. She'll help us get you up and to your room.'

The old woman was quiet but agitated, and a flash of what might be fear lit her eyes before she closed them again. Melissa was at a loss to understand why this had happened, and she suspected Harry was, too, although his demeanour remained calm.

★   ★   ★

158

Harry sat opposite Melissa at a highly polished mahogany table and watched with some satisfaction as she was able to grasp a knife and cut up the chicken his mama's cook had sent in.

'I was too late to ask them to chop the meats, but I think your strength is much restored,' he said.

'It is.' She smiled openly at him, and he returned it without dropping his gaze. 'I have been assiduous in following Zed's exercises.'

'That is good. Sometimes the patient works against our advice, and then the results are unpromising.'

'Will your mama be a good patient?'

'Mama is not as young as she appears, and occasionally she will keep to her room as she has this evening. I have to agree with her that rest is for her betterment. She sent word with her sincere apologies.'

'I take no offence, Colonel, but I do wonder why you are so very uneasy. If, as you say, your mother is aging, then a turn such as she had this afternoon must be expected. Is there something else? Has George been sighted?' She studied him with a steady gaze, and Harry had to hold his own.

She must have been formidable before the fire robbed her of her looks.

'I do not mean to criticise, but you have rearranged that wine glass more times than I could begin to count,' Melissa Pateley said, and laughed quietly.

Harry heard the tinkling sound and it squeezed his heart. She was never going to recover fully from the injuries, but the untouched side of her face remained beautiful, and the hair he'd seen growing through her damaged scalp was growing all over. She would soon be a personable young woman again; and if her limp continued to make her walking slow, then perhaps she would enjoy being on horseback.

More than all of the physical improvements he watched daily, her mental state was vastly different to the one he and Zed had encountered less than a week ago. She'd been on a threshold, he felt, and their challenging arrival had pitched her back into life in a way continued sequestration never would have.

'Colonel — Harry — what is it? What troubles you that these waves of pain cross your face?'

Harry blenched. How was it that the confidence he'd felt in Paxton's country house deserted him as soon as he returned to this bastion of female sisterhood? Perhaps Melissa Pateley would turn him down, but he would make it very difficult for her to do so. He drew himself up, and a smile eased his discomfort.

'I beg your pardon, Lady Pateley. May I call you Melissa?'

'Of course.' She blushed prettily. 'Given the intimacy of our early encounters, it would be silly to carry on in the formal manner.'

'Good. I will attend to your salve tonight, if I may. Zed has taken your girl, Joanie, off to look at one of our soap manufactories; and while Janet is as good a girl as mama employs, she is a little given to dramatics.' Harry held the countess's gaze as he spoke and was pleased to see the flash of recognition in her eyes. She knew that tonight would have a different ending, and she did not object.

They finished their meal. It was still early, and Harry offered Melissa his arm to take a stroll around the gardens in the middle of the square. Several of their neighbours were taking the air, and he introduced Lady Pateley as his mama's guest. She smiled graciously and soon had them at ease. If she made no reference to her damaged face, then they affected to be too well mannered to mention it.

Back in the house, Melissa went up to her room with one of the maids, and Harry waited till the girl came down again. He stopped her before she stepped off the bottom tread.

'Lady Pateley's injuries have made you shake, Bet. She will recover, but she won't ever look as she did before the fire in her London house.'

The girl dropped to the flags and dipped a curtsey. 'Thank ye, sir. It gied me a fricht, it did. But Lady Pateley wiz kind an said as how she was getting better an all.' She lifted the edge of her apron and wiped her eyes. 'Wiz it an accident, sir? The fire?'

'Lightning, I believe. Thank you, Bet. Joanie will be back soon.'

Harry watched the girl go down into the basement and listened for the snap of the door there before he laid a hand on the bannister and looked up. Was this wrong? He knew that a week ago, before he set eyes on his beautiful patient, he would have unequivocally said it was. Tonight, he was unable to prevent his feet lifting and taking the treads deliberately. Tonight, he would tell his patient she was recovered as far as he could help her, and that they must engage his mama's physician should she need more treatment. Tonight, he was crossing a line.

Melissa sat on an upright chair close to the bath with its rapidly cooling water. The little maid, Bet, had been very anxious to assist, but not able to stop the squeal of horror when Melissa's ravaged skin was fully exposed. She'd done her best to calm the girl, and later she'd heard Harry Gunn's measured tones floating up the stairwell. He always knew what was needed.

She answered the quiet tap on her door, and he came through. The white apron dangled from his right hand, and she saw him check around the room to make sure the roll of cotton was ready and the soaps and salves in their individual dishes.

'There seems to be a much wider selection of soaps,' she said, and heard the tremor in her voice. When she looked away, she was aware of the intensity of his gaze raking her, because her skin flared with heat.

'Yes, I keep a warehouse down in the

Grassmarket, and the manufactory Zed and Joanie have gone to visit also has storage.' He crossed the room and stripped off his evening jacket to expose the linen shirt. Long cuffs draped over the backs of his hands and drew Melissa's gaze to the covering of fine hairs growing through weather-browned skin.

'Your cuffs will suffer,' she said.

'Will it disturb you very much if I remove my shirt?'

The words reverberated around Melissa's head and she could not reply. She simply shook her head a little and hoped he would take it as permission. What did a lady do while her physician removed his own clothes?

No physician. We have gone beyond that and I am so very glad.

Harry draped his shirt over the back of a chair and came to stand in front of her. Muscles rippled below the bleached cotton garment that was all his protection now, and she watched the material move as he did. It was tucked into the top of his evening breeches, and she had to avert her eyes from the tell-tale bulge that garment both concealed and revealed.

Warmth stirred low in her belly where she had feared she would never have heat stirring again. Neville had been all she ever wanted, and his loss so devastating that she had stopped seeking such adventure.

Harry's warm hands slid around her waist and lifted her so she had to bend back to look into his eyes. She felt the trembling that shook his big frame. She felt the pressure of his arousal where it dug against her through the thin barrier of towelling.

'This is not the way I minister to any other of my patients,' he said, and she risked a chuckle.

'I would be most unhappy to discover I was an accommodation.'

'An accommodation, madam.' His words reflected his outrage. 'Do you think a landed gentleman, much decorated and more than solvent, needs to find accommodation?'

She laughed aloud and felt the tension ease from Harry's frame.

'Were you in better health, ma'am, that remark would certainly attract retribution,' he growled and brought his head down into the crook between her head and her collar-bone. One of his big hands cupped her bottom and she groaned as his fingers kneaded there.

'Surely, sir, a much decorated hero of the battlefield would not raise his hand to a lady?' Even as she teased him with her words, she leant into him, enjoying the heat smouldering between them.

'That would depend very much on the degree of provocation provided by the lady in question. In some circumstances, I see no argument against dealing with devilment by swatting her dignity.'

Harry eased the towel away from her shoulders, and she felt a cooling breeze tickle its way down her undamaged left side. He ran his hand across her right shoulder and down towards her waist.

That sensation was slight, even slighter than a tickle, but it was real. He was, however, examining, and she submitted in silence.

'I do think the skin is dry all over,' Harry said at last. 'Now, I need to ensure I do not dress it when the treatment would start up another and worse reaction.'

'You mean, it may be time to stop?'

'Yes. I am no longer principally your physician.'

His eyes held hers and his head came slowly down. She watched the skin around his mouth pucker a little and let her tongue escape to slide along her lips. Anticipation racked her body, making her grip the back of his head and pull him down to her. The kiss deepened so quickly Melissa had to cling hard onto Harry's big frame lest she fell away.

When the door opened, it was several seconds before either of them realised they were no longer alone.

9

'As soon as ye're done wi' Lady Pateley's burns, Harry, I'd welcome yer attendance in ma room.' Mrs Gunn's refined Edinburgh speech was stripped bare in her distress, but Melissa was still able to understand the words. She lifted panic-stricken eyes to Harry's face and shrank as she recognised the shame infusing his features.

The door closed and its latch rattled into place. Harry kept his arms around her and she was glad, because she knew her legs had lost the power to hold her upright.

'Melissa, Lady Pateley, I am so sorry.' His words came haltingly.

'Your mama may not have been so far into the room that she saw our kiss,' Melissa said, although whatever Mrs Gunn had seen or not seen must be capable of translation by a matron and mother of four.

'I don't think Mama will be in any doubt about what she was looking at, my dear. I am glad.' He eased her back and set her onto the chair she'd used earlier.

Melissa hoped he meant because they would not have to break the news of their attachment to his relatives, but the depth of sadness in Harry's darkening eyes warned her it was not what he meant.

'I am glad because I was entirely in the wrong to treat you in such a way.'

'Harry, I do not think of you as I do of the men who ministered to me in London and Newcastle. You have been punctilious in your dealings with me when I was still vulnerable . . . '

'Do not say any more, please. I cannot bear it.' He turned away, and Melissa saw his hand sweep across his eyes. Was he crying? Had this brought a hardened war physician to tears?

'Harry, I hear people moving below.

Perhaps Joanie has returned.'

'I will send her to you. Please believe me, Lady Pateley, I would not have had anything like this happen to you. I sincerely wish I had refused my uncle's pleas.' He strode from the room, and Melissa sat on staring at the panels of the door.

Refused his uncle's pleas? The words tumbled around her head. She did not for a single moment wish that any longer. George Gunn was still a dire threat to her wellbeing, although she knew her own uncles would now make sure that villain was kept at bay; but she began to think she could not breathe easily if separated from Harry. Whatever had brought shame to his face, she would deal with. He could not abandon her now, surely?

★   ★   ★

Harry paused on the landing. He took a moment to realise he'd left the countess's room without his shirt or coat; and when he did, he climbed the flight of stone stairs opposite him to his own room. An interval of calm would help him compose the strength of mind he needed before going back to face his mama. He pulled a neck cloth and fresh shirt from his drawers. A coat hung across the back of a chair and he eased himself into it. His mama was hardly going to comment on his appearance given the nature of what they must discuss. Finally, when he heard Joanie's sharp rap against the countess's door on the floor below, he knew he could hide from her displeasure no longer.

'Good evening, Mama,' he said. He was conscious of the words' formality and wondered if an English colonel would accompany them with a bow. He crossed the room and, drawing his mother out of her chair, wrapped his arms around her.

'It was madness, Harry, to go to her without one of the maids, or even Zed.' She trembled in his arms, but her voice was strong and her meaning clear.

'Mama, I know. She is like a madness. It fires my blood, and I think I have found something I've waited all my life for.' He set his mother back on her chair. They were alone, and the long summer evening was drawing to its close. Candles flared in the wall sconces and a lamp was lit on his mama's table.

'All your life,' Mrs Gunn mused. 'Harry, there are things in your past that I had hoped you would never know or need to know, but I cannot stand by. I would ask you to wait until Lottie comes in the morning, but I know that would be cruel.'

'Mama, I love you dearly.'

'I know, my boy. And your papa loved you, too. But sometimes love can trap a person,' she said quietly. Harry was grateful for her calm. He wasn't sure that he could have endured this if she'd been in a nervous vapour.

'Can I help, Mama? I know you blenched when you remembered how very flaxen I was as a child. I think this is because it reminded you of Lady

Pateley's own name, Flaxxe.'

'You must have been a formidable soldier, my dear. Your eye misses very little.' Mrs Gunn smiled. 'After Lottie was born, I delivered six sons to your papa, and they all died at birth or shortly thereafter. He did not know I was increasing when he went off to the Americas in 1786. I was ill. Too many babies and so little hope of another healthy outcome, I tended to ignore Lottie. That was an error of judgement I was to pay dearly over. She encountered Roland Farquar at the kirk, if you please.'

In his mind's eye, Harry saw the local church in Auchenwylde where the family worshipped when on their country estate. It was small, and a visitor would stand out. A handsome male visitor would easily catch the eye of a barely supervised schoolroom minx.

'Poor Lottie. Papa away. Mama all but bedridden, and in very low spirits when not.' Mrs Gunn paused. 'Suffice

174

it to say, she and he found a way to meet, and it soon became clear Lottie carried a memory of him. He disappeared within a matter of a month. We never saw him again, but there was no doubt who had done the deed.'

'No, I cannot imagine there would be,' Harry agreed. He sat down, too, and lifted his mama's hand to stroke it. 'When papa returned — ?'

His mama's exaggerated sigh reminded him of Lottie at her most dramatic. She shook her head as if trying to sort conflicting memories into some kind of order.

'There was much between then and your papa's return, but, in short, two baby boys were born. My son died within a week, but you, born a little early, survived — and Lottie . . . '

'Mama,' Harry said. The word brought tears into his mother's eyes, and he stared in dismay as they slid down her cheeks.

'Lottie persuaded me to take you as my own.'

'I *am* your own. I could never have wished for a better mama or papa,' Harry said. He wondered whether his papa had ever known of the deceit.

'It did not end there, of course. Gunn returned before we expected him. I was in very troubled spirits, and he took little time to winkle the truth from us both. He was more understanding of Lottie's wilfulness than I could have hoped for, but he did agree to the proposal. He told her she would have to give up all rights in you, and he recorded your name in the kirk records as his own — his and mine.'

'I am legally your son?' Harry felt the enormity of his parents' deception descend on his shoulders. How could he pursue Melissa Pateley or any respectable woman when he was a bastard by birth?

'Your papa had seen so much wrangling and misery over property claims in the New World that he insisted on it. His will was redrafted immediately. It meant one or two persons got to know about Lottie's fall from grace . . . '

'Fraser Duart's father was a lawyer,' Harry said, and a wealth of understanding flooded his brain. 'So Duart knows, too.'

'Yes, Duart knows. He had always admired Lottie, but she'd kept him at arm's length. When she began to interfere in your upbringing, your papa interfered in her life, too.'

Harry wondered whether he pitied the young Lottie. Did she deserve to be fobbed off on a man ten years her senior? The thought didn't trouble him for too long. No man her own age would have had the strength of mind and purpose needed to handle his sister. The word tripped him: sister, but not sister. Could he ever think of her in any other way?

'What happened to the dead baby?'

'He was given a name. The minister recorded him in the parish records as your twin.' Harry watched her twist a length of muslin around her slender fingers. 'We buried him in the orchard. As he had not been baptised . . . ' She hiccupped but continued . . . 'The minister raised no objections.'

They sat on as the candles burned down, and Harry felt curiously torn. He now understood so much of what had troubled him for many years.

★　★　★

Melissa stayed on the chair Harry had lowered her to for less than a minute, but it was sufficient to allow him an escape. She searched the room to find her wrapper. Clothes lay everywhere in jumbled heaps. Towels, the roll of cotton, even Harry's apron, and — she clapped cold fingers across her lips to seal the scream that rose unbidden — his shirt and evening coat.

She crossed the floor and lifted the shirt to bury her head in and inhale his scent as though she were picking it from a battlefield and would never encounter him again. That unhappy thought brought her head up, and she thrust the shirt under her pillow. If this was a battle, she was underarmed and disadvantaged. She needed to do something about that.

Another knock sounded on the door, and Joanie entered. The girl wore a pelisse of thin wool over her house-dress, and Melissa caught sight of a length of ribbon peeping from one of the pockets. Had that been prompted by Donal or Zed? she wondered.

'Joanie, is Colonel Gunn still up and about?' she asked.

'I didn't see him, my lady, but Janet told Zed that the maister — ' The girl rolled her tongue around the 'r', and Melissa smiled obligingly. ' — would be closeted with her mistress for some time.' Joanie said nothing else. Her eyes raked the room, and Melissa knew she would have to say something. Like any well trained lady's maid, Joanie would not ask; but she and the girl were now so close, it was out of the question to pretend nothing had happened here.

'Colonel Gunn came in after Bet helped me undress, Joanie. He made a final examination of my scars and has said there should be no further applications of salve.' She shivered. The towels were little protection against gathering night, and her wrapper was perversely still hidden.

'Did the girl not help you on with your night gown, my lady?' Joanie said, and clucked her displeasure. 'I would never have gone out with that Zed and Donal if the housekeeper hadn't said Bet would be sure to attend to you as she does Mrs Duart when she stays.'

Joanie began to bustle, and within minutes had found Melissa's night-gown, her wrapper and a thin woollen shawl to bring a bit of warmth to her mistress's body. Only then did she turn to the bathwater. Melissa saw her eyebrows lift as she realised the water was clean and unused.

'Colonel Gunn was called away and I did not bathe,' she said.

'No, my lady.'

'Joanie, does Zed say anything about Mrs Duart?'

'Mrs Duart, my lady?' Joanie let her gaze skitter away across the room to focus on a point of the panelling beside the fireplace.

Melissa's heart sank. She was sure Lottie Duart was at the heart of whatever was mysterious in this family. It was unthinkable for her to have recommended George's suit, and she must have spoken under severe provocation. Or duress. The words hit Melissa with the force of a mallet. Duress? Why would Lottie Duart feel any need to secure a husband for her?

'Mrs Duart is a frequent visitor to her mama, and the older servants behave as if she is the mistress sometimes. Mrs Gunn can be unhappy and suffer from nervous afflictions.' Joanie was moving around the room while she spoke, and it was a moment or two before Melissa understood the import.

'As the mistress?' she asked quietly.

'And yet, she has given up her room to allow the colonel to offer me hospitality.'

'Her husband has a castle on an island, my lady,' Joanie said. 'She also has a house in the New Town, as they call it here. Over the big lake.'

'The Nor Loch.'

'Them's the words. She doesn't go there too much because her mama-in-law doesn't like her above half.'

'We are gossiping, Joanie,' Melissa said, but could not draw the conversation to a close. What influence did Lottie have over her younger brother and her mama? The older servants were bound to have an inkling, and Joanie would by now have begun to learn what that was.

'My lady, the servants are loyal to the mistress, but sometimes her low moods make life hard for everyone, and that's maybe why Mrs Duart comes here so much. Her own boys are at school or in the university, so she's not needed at home much when her lord is away.'

Joanie came to a stand. Melissa realised she'd seen Harry's evening coat.

'The colonel left without his coat. Perhaps you would carry it out to Zed?' Joanie was to sleep in a small closet next to Melissa's room instead of with the other servants in the basement. 'They can get the bathwater in the morning. If George Gunn comes calling, I might drown him in it.'

Joanie dropped a curtsey and, retrieving Harry's coat, left the room. Melissa drew a deep breath, and after a moment or two crossed to the bed. Her fingers slid under the huge pillows and closed around Harry's shirt. His smell lingered on, and she felt tears on her cheek as she breathed it in. Hardly aware of her actions, Melissa stripped off her nightgown and pulled the shirt over her head. She clutched its folds and breathed again, allowing his smell to waft and console her for his absence.

Flaxxe. Melissa had never devoted much time to the origin of names. England had experienced so many waves of immigrants over hundreds of years that names were often stranger than one might expect. Smiths knew their origins. Wrights and Farmers, too. Did Flaxxe connect with flaxen? Was her family descended from people who'd come from the cool northern lands? Why was Mrs Gunn so upset when she brought Harry's babyish hair colour to mind?

Fifteen years is a long time for a person to be without any brothers or sisters when their parents are still married. Some girls are old enough at fifteen to be in their own marriage. Some girls of strong but undisciplined character might go against all the good sense and good breeding of their family. People thought that I had done those things at seventeen when I married Neville. That's the difference, of course — the wedding ceremony.

Her thoughts did not please her as she climbed into the bed. Harry Gunn was a formidable gentleman of good family. What if his position was all built on a lie? How would she feel about that? How would she feel? Melissa chewed her bottom lip. She suspected Harry Gunn would want to give up his pursuit of her through a misguided sense of honour.

Damn honour and all its wrong-headed applications.

10

'Donal,' Melissa said as she entered the ground floor room Simmerton had brought her to the following morning, 'is your master in the house?'

Melissa had lain awake long into the night. She'd heard the neighbours' sons return as a hall clock struck three deep clangs. She'd heard them finally separate and enter their homes as it chimed the half. Sometime around then, she'd removed Harry's shirt and replaced it with her nightgown. It was still only ten now, but the table was set for several places, and she hoped Harry had not broken his fast early and departed.

'The maister, ma'am? He and the sergeant left over an hour ago. Mistress Gunn will be down shortly.' Donal stood behind a chair and Melissa obligingly sat in it. Together they managed to push and pull it into the table. 'The maister said to remind you that Mistress Duart will be calling later with Mistress Gordon and Mistress Ramsay.'

Melissa could not bring herself to look up at the young man. She was sure her complexion had fired, and wondered how long she would react whenever Lottie Duart's name was mentioned.

When I remember how important the woman is in this family, I am going to be hard pressed. It is time to get hold of these vapourish reactions and take stock.

'She made the arrangement yesterday, Donal. I do remember, thank you.'

Melissa accepted some porridge, and when she was wondering whether she could ask Donal for the sugar basin, a long arm snaked around her and sprinkled brown crystals over her bowl.

Harry. His scent teased her. His large frame between her back and the window cut down the light and threw shadows over the board. The silver spoon caught a single ray of sunlight and sparkled. Melissa sat rigid. He had returned?

'I am sorry no one was here to welcome you, ma'am. My mother keeps to her room until midday, although she did intend to rise this morning. I had business at the soap works which could not wait.'

'Ah well,' Melissa said. 'A captive cannot dictate when her abductors will attend to her, can she?'

'No, but I hope, now we are in the city and under my family's roof, you will regard yourself as a guest rather than a captive,' Harry said equably. He refused the challenge she was throwing to him, and it annoyed her tired and overwrought sensibilities.

'Is that what you hope, Colonel?' She felt the breeze as he moved away from her chair back and heard Donal's startled intake of breath. 'Now we are in the city, I think it will be more suitable for me to find respectable lodgings in order that I might make arrangements for my return to New-castle.'

'Oh, so you discount a return to Berwick Old Abbey?' he said, and the laughter lurking behind his words inflamed her temper.

'Of course I do. Do you think I've learned nothing about the behaviour of your relatives? Eccentric some might say, but others might use criminal.' Melissa set her spoon on the cloth and was irritated further by the trembling of her hand.

'Donal.'

Harry waited till the younger man had left and clipped the door closed behind him before he laid two warm and strong hands on her shoulders. Tremors raced down her arms and heat suffused her.

'Have you worked it out?' The question was stark, and his voice cut through the hours of wasted time when she'd speculated over the events of yesterday.

'Yes, I believe I have.' She took a

189

deep breath and spoke the words that should never have to be said in any respectable family. 'Lottie gave birth, and her parents subsequently entered the baby in all records as their own.'

She felt his fingers constrict, and clamped her lips on a tiny squeal that rose within. So it was as she had thought. Lottie was Harry's mother and not his sister. Yet, was it not the case that she was both?

'Who else knows of this?' Melissa asked in a quieter voice. She could see that after such a long time, it would be hard to unravel what really took place.

'Very few. Lottie's late papa-in-law was the lawyer my father used, so her husband knows, and possibly her mama-in-law . . . ' Harry trailed off.

'You are perhaps thinking that is why Mrs Duart is not loved by her mama-in-law?' Melissa spoke without thinking. He would know she'd been listening to servants' gossip.

'Aye, it occurs to me that might be the cause of their animosity. And who can blame her?'

Silence hung between them, and Melissa wondered how long it might continue when the rattle on the street door sounded. It was a cheeky and cheerful sound, as if the persons waiting were impatient to come in and meet with them.

'You should eat that porridge, my dear. If Kitty and Mairie are in their usual spirits, it may be some time before any further food is available to you.'

Melissa ate as instructed while people milled outside in the hall. Her brain felt as if it had been split into two. One set of responses was shrouded in a cloud of indecision and near desperation. The other was crystal clear. In life it had been good to be governed by the laws of the land; but on the other hand, there was no second son in the Gunn family to be displaced or robbed of his birthright by Harry. The fraudulent records had been created by two men who were now dead; and what purpose could be served by dragging their names into disrepute? No wonder at all that Mrs Gunn and Lottie had remained silent.

Melissa swallowed the unfamiliar porridge. It was warm and comforting. She drank a cup of coffee and set her shoulders back. Recovery this morning seemed much closer to hand than it had been for the weeks of her seclusion. She wanted Harry Gunn, and she would have him.

★   ★   ★

'Lady Pateley,' Lottie Duart greeted as she came into the breakfast room. Harry sat across the table and raised a challenging glance towards the rush of ladies joining them. He might just have learned two of the young women were his aunts, but he showed no sign of succumbing to intimidation in their presence.

'Lottie, Kitty, Mairie,' he spoke with deliberation, and the advance slowed a little. 'I have explained to Lottie that although Lady Pateley is much recovered from her injuries, she is not as robust as she will be, but perhaps I need to say it again.'

'Fiddlesticks, brother,' one of the new visitors said, and Melissa quailed. They had not discussed whether or how much was known by these people. This lady either had not been told, or had and was not yet used to the new knowledge.

She raised stricken eyes to Harry and he smiled. How delightful it would be to be entitled to see that smile every morning, she thought.

'I say fiddlesticks, too, Harry. Lottie has kept Kitty and myself in the dark over the dreaded George's abhorrent behaviour, and we will not be further delayed.'

'Delayed?' Harry asked, and raised a quizzical eyebrow. 'Are you rushing off again? You have only just crossed Mama's threshold.'

'Don't be obtuse. Mairie and I are in

town for three weeks at least while our lords shoot everything that moves on their ground. Uncle John has made us most welcome, but clearly the real life is being lived here.' A young woman with Mrs Gunn's spare frame and unusual height moved round the edge of the table and, pulling out a chair, sank into it. She was possessed of sparkling eyes that drew the gaze to her, and when she had secured Melissa's she smiled with real warmth. 'When are you going to introduce me to Lady Pateley? For I know Mama will expect us to observe London formalities.'

'And me?' the other newcomer asked. She, too, found a chair and sat down. Melissa thought she was shorter than her sisters and a little plumper.

'Lady Pateley,' Harry began, and Melissa turned back to him, 'may I present my sisters, Mrs Lamont Gordon and Mrs Hector Ramsay. We call them Kitty and Mairie.' His sisters rose again and dropped polite curtseys.

'Harry, perhaps the ladies would call

me Melissa. I am so glad to meet them and to discover George Gunn has other normal relatives.' She did not attempt to return the ladies' curtseys because it would involve struggling up out of her chair, but bestowed warm smiles on both. She turned to Lottie. 'Lottie, it is good to see you again, and kind of you to bring your sisters.'

Lottie Duart looked a little surprised by Melissa's use of her given name, but one glance at Harry's shuttered expression appeared to put her off asking whether she was forgiven for her promotion of George, and she simple dipped a polite curtsey before taking a seat.

'My mama is still in her room?' she asked. Harry nodded. 'I will go up to her in a few moments, but first I must find out whether Lady Pateley slept comfortably.'

'Thank you, ma'am. I was very comfortable, although I did not sleep until after three o'clock. I fear the excitements of the last days are taking a toll.' Melissa did not look at Harry, as she feared her reaction to his expression would be the undoing of her. The ladies would hardly expect fits of giggles from a widow of such standing.

'Would you be more comfortable in an establishment of your own?' Lottie asked, and Melissa did look at Harry then. They all did, because his exclamation of irritation was both loud and intense.

'What kind of suggestion is that, ma'am?' he growled.

'I wonder whether you or your sisters know of any agent trying to rent out something suitable,' Melissa asked, cutting across Harry's intervention. She was loth to be living alone while George was on the loose, but she had already thrown the idea at Harry's large head in anger herself.

'There are no suitable houses available, Melissa,' Harry snapped.

'Goodness, Harry, have you been looking to engage a house?'

Melissa heard the thread of steel

weaving Lottie's words together. She still wanted to drive a wedge between them and was prepared to risk open argument in its pursuit. Was that an incentive to stay put in George Square, where she could see these machinations at first hand?

'Don't believe we have vanquished George simply because we have not seen him. Melissa knows how little evidence that gives of his whereabouts.'

Melissa heard the sharp intakes of breath his younger sisters made, but did not turn to them. Lottie may have glanced their way looking for support, however, because one of them spoke.

'Why, Lottie, Mrs Merryweather is looking to find a careful tenant for her house on Queen Street. Mairie and I were taking tea with her granddaughter yesterday afternoon and she mentioned it.'

'The Merryweather house is new and well appointed, I believe,' Lottie said thoughtfully. Melissa watched how her eyes strayed to Harry's face and began to hold a careful expression. 'Why do you say George may not be vanquished, Harry? He is a gentleman, and having heard the countess's opinion on his suit, will have retreated.'

'I think not.' Harry was on his feet and moving round the table to stand behind her chair. Melissa thought she could feel the force of his anger. 'I would have a word with you in private, Melissa. Perhaps you would like to walk around the square?'

'No, sir, I don't think I would. Can Mrs Merryweather's house be viewed today, do you think?' she asked Kitty and Mairie. She had not formed any real intention of moving and then moving again to Newcastle so abruptly. There had been more than enough flitting about for a person trying to recover from illness. It was rather satisfactory, however, to tweak Harry's tail.

'Melissa!'

'There is no need to treat our house

guest to a demonstration of parade-ground manners,' Lottie said. 'Melissa has made it clear she does not wish to go anywhere with you.'

'I thank you to keep your elegant nose out of my affairs, sister.'

Melissa watched Lottie's complexion fire and at the same time thought a little of the life went out of her eyes. She was conscious of the shocked silence this exchange was causing Kitty and Mairie. Perhaps it would be wiser to agree to walk with Harry rather than insist on having her own way.

She reached across the old damask cloth and squeezed Lottie's fingers. They were cold and the woman shook a little.

'Very well, sir. I will take a turn around the square with you.'

＊　＊　＊

Harry held the front door wide and watched Melissa carefully negotiate the two deep steps onto the platt. She waited for him and he offered his arm. It was a trial to have her so close, but they would look odd walking separately around the square when every neighbour knew who she was and how badly injured she had been.

The warmth of her body teased his senses, and he thought in those few moments before he brought her into the shade of the gardens that he might go mad. His life had been a model of service and rectitude. What offence had he committed that the Gods were treating him in this way? he wondered. Would she ever be able to see beyond the slur of his bastard status? Not that it mattered, because he could never marry now and perpetuate the wrong.

'Why are you so tense, sir?' Her voice was laced with anxiety. 'Surely you cannot think I can continue in your household with my servants taking up space and your sisters confined to their uncle's house?'

'Melissa, you are being as obtuse as possible. George Gunn is out there watching your every move, and it cannot be safe for you to live alone.'

'I will write to my aunt in Newcastle later today and suggest that she send one or other of her sons to accompany me on the return trip. If I need to take a house for a month or two, then my cousin can live with me.'

'And why would you need to live in Edinburgh at all if this paragon of an aunt is in Newcastle and willing to play host to you?' He suspected Melissa wasn't being as straightforward as she might in referring to the aunt. 'Besides, you can be honest with me. I understand that news of my irregular parenting must make you wish to put as much distance as possible between us.'

'What? How can you say such a thing? I have known you as a person before learning of this, what did you call it, irregularity? Do you think I am shallow? Do you think, like the blaggard Withershaws, that I hang out looking for suitors of aristocratic lineage?'

The vehemence of Melissa's response

stopped Harry in his tread. Had he misunderstood her wish to live apart from his family? Was he so overwhelmed by the discovery of Lottie's fall from grace and its implications that he was pressing his reservations on her?

'You were mightily responsive to Lottie's suggestion.'

'I . . . ' She trailed off, and he glanced down at the mounting colour covering her features. 'I was simply tweaking the lion's tail.'

'Really?' Harry heard the feebleness of his question, but saw that the lady was too overcome by being found in the wrong that she passed it over. 'That was unkind, ma'am.'

'Oh, Harry, do not 'ma'am' me, please. I agree. It was unkind, and I deserve your censure.'

'Were we able to be private, there might be more than words supporting my annoyance,' he ventured, and surprised himself with its audacity. How unsettling it was to be blown hot and then cold by a woman. He had much to learn. 'Your aunt?' He deliberately brought the conversation back to a safer topic.

'My aunt and I deal well enough, sir, but undoubtedly we deal better when a carriage ride separates our establishments.' She stopped and drew a small circle in the dirt of the path with her shoe. 'My relatives did not approve of my marriage, and while we have improved our dealings a lot, they do not yet amount to living together.'

'They left you vulnerable after the fire,' Harry pointed out, and heard Melissa's sharp intake of breath.

'Yes, but I do not think they understood how difficult my relations with Withershaws had been or how intense George Gunn's interest in me is. I cannot blame them. I did go against all advice in marrying Neville as I did.' Harry heard the pride in that remark and thought how a father would itch to take the miss to task. Of course Melissa was an orphan by the time she married Neville Pateley, and no doubt her uncles were less inclined to deal with her as she deserved.

'It is very well for you to keep up this bravado, but it was a foolhardy thing to do.' Harry regretted the words as soon as he uttered them. At his side, Melissa drew in a sharp breath, and he knew she was angry. Too late. 'Neville Pateley turned out to be a good and decent man. It cannot have been clear that he was to your relatives.' She let out her pent-up breath, and Harry recognised her defeat.

'No,' she said quietly. 'I do not argue this point with you, sir. I was seventeen and in love. Foolhardiness was part of the whole.'

'I beg your pardon, ma'am. I have no right . . . '

'Please, Harry, again you 'ma'am' me. I will certainly have a relapse. In return I will allow that I was humouring your sister and have no wish to live alone while your mad cousin is out there untrammelled.' He sensed the depth of despair and it fired every male fibre. What a muddle. What an unholy muddle.

'I was, however, right in my assessment of Neville's character.'

'Yes, you were. More so than your uncles have been in Mr Withershaws's. I acknowledge that.' He eased their pace and brought Melissa to a bench where they might sit.

'I would be glad to remain under your roof if you do not dwell on the circumstances of your birth.'

Harry felt his insides curdle. All his life he had lived under the shadow of a strong and powerful woman whose hold on him was now revealed. Despite his new knowledge of her relationship to him, Harry was conscious that Lottie could cause a great deal of trouble should she decide to reveal his parentage.

'Lottie may be a greater obstacle to your purposes,' he said, and watched the colour flare across Melissa's undamaged left cheek. He stilled the hand that came up involuntarily to caress her. She gazed down at it and then pulled back her shoulders.

'Harry, you have been to war, and I have been in troubles that have tried me sorely. It seems to me that together we make a team fit to defeat the Lotties of this world.'

'My dear, would that it were so simple. Do you have any idea how hard we will find it to live so close and yet so separated?'

'Are you now arguing I should seek out Mrs Merryweather's man of business?'

Harry stood and offered his arm to Melissa while he thought over his words. 'No. It would be tantamount to offering George an open invitation. You must write to your aunt for an escort south; and while you are here, I will be out and about in my manufactories as much as possible.' He moved onto the gravel of the path and she was forced to move with him. 'Some of our family are lawyers, and perhaps we can have them study Withershaws's arguments. The law is different between England and Scotland, but much of how law operates will be similar, I think.'

'It would certainly make my life much easier if I could prise the family's affairs out of Withershaws's hands.'

'Then we will both be occupied,' Harry added as calmly as he could. 'And we need not fret over the possibility that an unsuitable attraction might grow between us.'

She took a few steps at his side before he heard her quiet words. 'And I do know how very hard it will be, Harry Gunn.'

11

Melissa settled into a routine of sorts while she waited for her aunt's reply. She was sitting on a bench in the gardens of the square one morning when Lottie Duart came striding along the gravel. Melissa still regarded the woman as a loose cannon, but on the occasions they met, had kept her conversation civil and unthreatening. She knew from Harry that Lottie had been told by her mama of his conversation with her.

'Good morning, Lottie. You look well in that shade. Pink suits your colouring, I think.' She watched with interest as Harry's sister blushed a little.

'Why, thank you, ma'am. I am so used to hearing no comment on my clothes in my male household that it is pleasant to hear a compliment.' She sat on Melissa's bench and stretched her legs in front of her for a moment before drawing them neatly back. 'I passed Harry in the high street. He was hurrying to a visit with our family lawyers.'

'I'm afraid my quarrel with Mr Withershaws exercises him more than a little,' Melissa replied mildly. She knew Harry was pursuing one or two ideas, perhaps more vigorously than she had hoped. The greater the vigour, the earlier a result might be expected. The earlier a result, the sooner he might expect her to remove to the south.

'I see. Harry did say that Uncle John had made several good suggestions. He remains insulted by a letter he received from the Withershaws person, although he does not disclose its content to me.' Lottie smoothed the folds of her gown. Out of the corner of her right eye, which was so much better now, Melissa saw two of Harry's casual guard patrolling. Lottie had come into the square alone, but she suspected Kitty and Mairie would not be very far behind her.

'It is kind of them both. We women are hampered by the restrictions placed on our sex,' Melissa replied. 'Perhaps Harry will have made some headway before I go south to my Aunt Flaxxe in Newcastle.'

'You have not received a reply to your request?'

'Not yet, no. Aunt Jayne is sometimes from home. I have many cousins, and they seek her help with birthing and advice on family illnesses.'

'You may have some time to wait then if one of your cousins has claimed her attentions first,' Lottie mused.

'I may. How can I compete with the birth of a grandchild?' Melissa wondered whether she would be glad if her aunt were from home. It was exquisitely painful to be so close to Harry and yet prevented from being close with him. If her aunt agreed to offer her a haven while she healed and while the family thought of a way to frustrate George Gunn, would she never see Harry again?

'A frown creases your expression, ma'am. Do you wish to extend your stay among us?' Lottie spoke slowly, and Melissa was aware of how carefully she chose her words.

'Lottie, may I ask you a painful question before I answer yours?'

'Painful questions have a habit of driving wedges into even secure friendships; and we, ma'am, are only making the acquaintance of each other.'

'I believe you are right, and apologise for any embarrassment my suggestion may have caused,' Melissa said. She saw the frown now creasing Lottie's brow and wondered whether curiosity would be the woman's undoing. If all Harry said about her was true, then she did not enjoy being without control over her surroundings and relatives. Information was a large part of that kind of control.

Melissa waited.

'Of course, were you to understand that I might reserve the right not to answer your question, then I would be prepared to hear it,' Lottie blurted.

'Why, that is a good way forward, Lottie. My question concerns my marriage.' She saw that this was not what Lottie had expected to hear. 'My relatives condemned it without exception. This is why I have to make overtures to my Aunt Flaxxe and not simply descend on her household.'

'Your marriage? Of course, it was reported in the scandal sheets at the time. While I do not read any such, one heard snippets, I'm afraid,' Lottie said with some hesitation.

'Indeed it was. It was also reported in respectable papers, so it's unsurprising that you read of it. What I wonder is whether you understand.' Melissa watched the words curl around Lottie's guarded expression. She was appealing to her as a woman who had been overwhelmed by sentiment herself. Could they find a way through such shared experience to start unravelling the tangle of misery caused by Harry's parentage?

'Whether I understand?' Lottie murmured.

'Yes. Do you know what it feels like to think you will never draw another breath unless your desire to be held and — '

'Lady Pateley!' Lottie's complexion had fired, and beads of sweat collected along her upper lip so that she was forced to lick them away with her tongue.

Melissa sat still and quiet. She was putting the other woman under enormous pressure, but it was so very important to make common ground with her.

'I was a schoolroom miss, and no doubt if Mama had been in good health, I would not have had the opportunity to run wild that I took such advantage of.' Lottie spoke the words quietly, but without any pity for her younger self. 'If my papa had been in the country, Roland Farquar would not have succeeded in his dastardly pursuit.'

'All these things are true, Lottie; but I appeal to you. Do you understand what it is like to want — '

'Of course I do. I was running mad with the need to be in his arms,' Lottie interrupted. 'You are unkind, ma'am, to pine me with your questions as if I were a butterfly on your specimen board.'

'Unkind? We have both known a great love and lost him. You did love this man?'

'I thought I did. At the time, I thought I did, but I was very young.'

'Only two years younger than I, when I ran off with Neville.' Melissa let Lottie think about that for a moment or two. 'The difference in our lives comes from the fact that Neville was the Earl of Pateley and able to marry me.'

'A lady would naturally defend her husband's honour. I do not hold that against you, Lady Pateley.' Lottie sighed. Melissa waited, suspecting that she had more to say if given opportunity.

'Roland Farquar was tall and blond-haired with deep-set eyes that snapped with intelligence. He was a slim man, but strong. I thought at the time he might ride to hounds. His conversation was like nothing I had heard before.' Lottie's expression became dream-like. 'He taught me to play piquet. I believe he was rather good at it.'

'My papa was very good at card games, and piquet was a particular favourite of his,' Melissa said. The other's hazel gaze swept over her with an intensity Melissa found unsettling. She shivered despite the heat of the midday sun.

★   ★   ★

'I caught sight of you deep in conversation with Lottie.' Harry Gunn came upon her when she was least expecting an interruption, and Melissa jumped. Strong arms circled her waist and lifted her onto the first landing of the staircase. 'Beg your pardon,' he said, and she took note of the struggle he was having not to laugh aloud. 'I should remember you're expecting George to materialise out of blanket boxes and stairhead cupboards.'

Melissa took a deep and steadying breath as Harry's hands slid from her person. Did she detect a touch of reluctance? She gave herself a mental shake. How could she go on living in this shaded world of hidden truths and barely suppressed longing? It caught the breath in her throat and made her a difficult mistress. More than once, she'd snapped at Simmerton and injured the old man's feelings.

'Yes, sir; I was enjoying the early sunshine when she chanced on me and we exchanged some conversation.' She knew it was pompous and stiff, but she could hardly tell Harry she'd spent the time prising details of his mother's love affair from her.

'Really?' Harry was never going to be easily fooled or set aside. 'I must wonder what conversation reduces my formidable sister to wiping her eyes on the sleeve of her gown.'

'You noticed that?' Melissa asked.

'Playing for time, ma'am?'

'As you say. How did your meeting with the lawyers progress? Lottie thought it might relate to my affairs, which is why I ask.' She stood to one side and allowed Harry to open the door of the drawing room for her. He smelled of the sea today, and she wrinkled her nose. 'Why do you smell so powerfully of seaweed?'

'What a featherbrain you can be, ma'am, asking me about smells when your whole family's livelihood is at stake.' Harry gazed down at her and she held it as best she could. The hazel depths of his eyes were surely made for seduction, but perhaps this was not the time to think so.

'Featherbrain? How dare you?' Melissa sparred. It was a fair comment, and she could hardly refute it.

'Oh, I dare.' Melissa wondered whether, if their circumstances were different, would he dare so much more? He ushered her into the big room with its three windows facing the square. His mother and Lottie were already there, and a tray of coffee and tiny shortbread biscuits was set out. The ladies had sewing, but their attention was only a little to it. Both were trying to catch the gist of the conversation between Harry and Melissa. She sighed.

'Good afternoon, Mrs Gunn, Lottie,' she said, and smiled as best she could. The muscles in her face still protested if she tried to talk too much or smile too much or even eat. Recovery continued to be a slow process.

'Melissa was wondering why I smell so strongly of the sea.'

'She may find there are worse effects than seaweed when you're at your experiments,' Mrs Gunn said. 'He will have been attempting to make soap imbued with seaweed, my dear.'

'I see,' Melissa murmured, although she wasn't sure she did. 'Does seaweed make soap more . . . ' She let the words trail away because she could not think what seaweed did to soap.

'More something, but we do not have all the answers as yet,' Harry said equably. 'Unfortunately, my meeting with our lawyers ran over a little, and I didn't get far enough into the experiment. May I pour some coffee for you?'

'I am sorry if my affairs are distracting you, sir.'

'Don't be. I can shred seaweed on almost any day of the week, but I hardly ever get the opportunity to cross intellectual swords with anyone. I had forgotten how stimulating that can be.' He lifted the coffee pot and Melissa nodded. She watched the stream of hot liquid splash into Mrs Gunn's delicate china. It would still be difficult for her to lift a full silver pot, but she had the deep sense of that being about to change.

'Your friends, the Paxtons, have left invitations, Harry,' his mama said, and everyone turned to her. 'They seek our company this evening for the meal and

219

to play cards thereafter. I don't know how to reply. Lady Pateley, do you feel up to an evening among strangers?'

'Why, I think perhaps I do,' Melissa said, and her spirits rose again. 'But we did not have long to pack at Berwick Old Abbey. Will my trunks contain any garment suitable?'

'Agnes Paxton is always very elegant,' Lottie said doubtfully. 'But she is a gracious hostess and would never make you feel out of place. She always enjoys conversation.'

'I think that's true. I am hardly an expert on female fashion, ma'am, but Lottie is correct when she says Agnes enjoys company. I think whatever Joanie is able to present you in will be suitable.' Harry threw back the contents of his coffee cup and rose. He bowed to the ladies. 'I am expected back in the workshop to oversee something. I hope you may excuse me till the evening, Mama. I will of course escort you all to the Paxtons' house.'

They watched him leave, and Melissa

at least thought how neatly he had extricated himself. She sipped her own coffee and found she wished to know whether Harry Gunn had burned his tongue while drinking his.

It's the least he deserves. He never did answer my question about the meeting with the lawyers.

★ ★ ★

Melissa smoothed the front of her gown that evening while she drew a deep breath and glanced up again. Colonel Thomas Paxton was a big man and towered over the diminutive figure of his wife. Agnes smiled. Her welcome was warm and her words bubbled over like champagne escaping from its bottle.

'Lady Pateley, I am so delighted to make your acquaintance at last. When Thomas told me you were to be staying in The Keep, I had palpitations.' The lady spread her small fingers across the front of her gown where she would feel her heart thundering in her ribcage if she were indeed in the grip of palpitations.

Melissa smiled and already knew the tension she'd been experiencing before meeting these dearly held friends of Harry's was ebbing. Mrs Paxton thought her house was less than perfect for their visit.

'Why, ma'am, your house *was* perfection, and after a night — '

'For the night . . . ' Harry interrupted, and Melissa cast a sideways glance toward him. His mama and sisters had already gone off to converse with the few other guests scattered around the drawing room.

'Yes, for the night,' she ended lamely, and was not surprised by the puzzlement in Agnes Paxton's expression. 'Everything in your home in Duns is welcoming to the guest.' *Has he even kept Thomas and Agnes ignorant of our actual timetable?* she wondered.

'I am very glad for it,' the petite brunette, said and Melissa realised with a start that she meant every word. The bubbly personality and the conventional words did not quite disguise her real hope that her house had looked after its guests as if she'd been there. Melissa suddenly understood why Harry prized the friendship of his brother officer and his wife so highly. They cared for him.

'We did, however, have a minor intrusion from my distant cousin — whose behaviour, ma'am, is a little unpredictable,' Harry addressed Agnes Paxton, and Melissa did not miss the flash of understanding in the lady's eyes. 'I am sorry to have to tell you that a door was damaged as a result.'

'I am sorry, too, Gunn,' Agnes replied, but she did not probe. 'I expect Zed had it dealt with.'

'Indeed,' Harry said, and bowed over his hostess's hand. 'I am sorry for it though, and wish I had been able to forestall George.'

They agreed over the desirability of that, and then Agnes steered the conversation to more mundane matters before her butler called the party to dinner. Melissa was glad to have heeded Lottie's advice about a shawl as the evening progressed. Although fires were lit in the drawing room before they returned to it, the colonel's ancient mansion was huge, and draughts, even on a summer evening, found gaps in the woodwork around the windows.

'Lady Pateley,' Agnes said as Harry followed some of the other men out of the room, 'I hope you will sit here and tell me how you find Edinburgh. These men are mostly likely setting up a card table or two.' The woman patted the sofa beside her. 'I believe this is your first visit to our capital?'

'Thank you, ma'am. It is my first visit, and unexpected, too.' Melissa let the distracted words escape, and only when Agnes Paxton's eyebrows lifted did she realise her mistake. 'I mean Mrs Gunn — '

'I think, Lady Pateley, I have an idea of what you mean, but there are a few here who might misconstrue,' Agnes whispered. More loudly she added, 'It is always so hard to know when visits will suit, particularly if the weather has been wet. We often find the roads around the Keep turn into deep mud that traps our carriage wheels and discourages one from venturing out.'

Melissa smiled. She was puzzled. Harry had clearly assumed Agnes would not have been told of her abduction from Berwick and their night under canvas. Or had he? she wondered. She raised her head lazily and glanced around the well dressed gathering. Was there one, or more than one, who would carry tales? she wondered. As if sensing her confusion, Agnes spoke again very quietly.

'It is always wise to assume some among one's friends will be a little loose in their morals and might carry information to the scandal sheets. Not all have quite enough to live on, you know, ma'am. They can supplement their income by supplying tittle-tattle from the drawing rooms to which they have an entrée.'

Melissa knew her own brows rose in consternation. 'Of course, it is so in London and Bath.' She thought the matter over. George might be prepared to pay for information, too. Withershaws certainly would. Her blood chilled.

All too soon, Melissa saw Mrs Gunn rise from her chair and her daughters follow suit. She stood up too, and was well pleased to be able to do so without requiring the arm of a footman. She knew Percy was awaiting instructions in the servants' quarters, and Mrs Gunn's footman, too, was in their party.

'Mrs Gunn,' Agnes said, 'it was so kind of you to bring your party along this evening, and I hope your cook is not put out by the short notice.'

'No, she is not, Agnes. Indeed, I heard mutterings among the staff about the quality of the catch brought round from Leith and Musselburgh this morning. So perhaps she was relieved.'

Mrs Gunn smiled, but Melissa saw the lines of strain around the older woman's eyes. Her own presence in her house was clearly making heavy demands. Maybe her aunt would write soon and offer some solution to the impasse.

'Ah, yes. You would notice the meal did not include any fish, which is a great pity; but my cook was also wary of what was being offered.' Agnes moved toward the door as her guests began to group themselves for departure. Melissa wondered whether word had been sent to the card tables.

In the lobby, with its aged wooden block floors and painted walls, lamps and candles burned. Melissa saw Percy and Simmerton waiting on the front steps as she accepted help with her pelisse of thick cotton. It was warm enough for the evening air, despite the haar that began to swirl up from the seashore, and the relatively short walk back to Harry's house. Thomas, their host, was not in sight. Harry and Zed were missing, too. In fact, none of the husbands were present, and a murmur of irritation arose among the other wives. The Gunn ladies, however, took their leave of their hostess with warm thanks and no comments about the missing escorts.

Perhaps Harry forgets his filial duties when once immersed in a card game, she thought. That made her trip slightly over the edge of a step. Did she want Harry's character to be formed in the mould of a card player?

'Thank you, Simmerton. I lost sight of the steps beyond the hem of my gown.' Melissa regained her balance with help from her man, but not her equilibrium. She supposed it was possible for a man to inherit skills and passions from a dead parent he'd never met. How did it improve anything if Harry Gunn was a gambler?

12

The letter from her aunt arrived the following morning, and Melissa took it from Simmerton's tray when she came downstairs first thing. She could hear voices behind the dining parlour door. One was certainly deeper than the ladies of the household, but not Harry.

Her thoughts of Harry were clouded this morning. He had honoured his promise to escort the ladies to Colonel Paxton's house, but deserted them without ceremony or even the briefest of explanations. It was too bad of him, and Melissa suspected he did know more than he was allowing her to know of Mr Withershaws's activities. Clearly he'd wanted to avoid her, and kept himself aloof from further questioning. That was a slightly more palatable explanation than the thought that he was in thrall to the tables.

Melissa glanced at the spidery scrawl across her letter. There was no mistaking its origin; besides, her cousin William had franked it for his mama. She folded it into four and stuffed it into the neck of her morning gown below her shawl. If Simmerton raised an eyebrow, she chose not to observe it.

Once inside the dining parlour, Melissa saw that their small family had increased and Mrs Gunn had risen from her bed early. A stranger, another tall man, rose slowly from his chair and studied Melissa across the breadth of the table. He narrowed his gaze and pursed his lips in a manner that reminded Melissa of several of her elderly aunts. There was no mistaking the intelligent gleam of understanding that flooded his eyes before he dropped the lids to conceal it.

'My lady,' he said in a strong Highland accent. 'And it is to be hoped the noise of women chattering did not disturb your dreams after a night at the Paxtons' house. I know myself, and sometimes to my cost, how demanding such a visit can be.'

'Why no, sir. I always wake around the same hour, and today was no different.'

'Then I am glad to be acquainted with that information, ma'am. Henny, perhaps you would be making a formal introduction between me and the countess?' The gentleman turned towards Mrs Gunn, and Melissa realised with a start that Harry had been called for her and not his papa or grandpapa. Did the lady look as she would expect a Henrietta to look? she wondered.

'It's very well for you to be complaining, Uncle John. But you're already delving into Lady Pateley's sleeping habits and talking as if some person had turned a clockwork screw in your back . . . '

'Hush, my dear, hush. I accept all of your criticisms. I have no manners to speak of, living as I do in the isolation of a woman-free household.'

'Your household currently contains my eldest daughter and her sisters. They have all been dining with you regularly while their menfolk are from town.' Mrs Gunn was irritable beyond anything Melissa had observed in the few days she'd been staying under the lady's roof, and it piqued her interest. What information had her late husband's uncle brought with him? Or what questions had he been asking?

'Mrs Gunn, I am delighted to make the acquaintance of Harry's uncle. Good morning, sir.' She dropped a tiny curtsey and was relieved to be able to keep her balance, although she saw Donal's careful observation out of the corner of her left eye. He'd followed her into the room, having knocked loudly and rattled the door-handle as he opened it to allow her to pass. *Oh yes,* she thought, *secrets are being traded here this morning.*

Donal came forward then and drew a chair out from the table that she might sit down. He brought her a bowl of fresh porridge and a cup of fragrant coffee. Melissa thought of her aunt's letter nestling in her bosom and of the carefully measured portions doled out in Newcastle when she had visited with her parents. The one did not compare very favourably with the other. Raising her spoon to her lips, she then allowed a silence to grow around her. When were the old people going to jump in?

'Yes,' Uncle John said. 'Likewise, I am most pleased to make your closer acquaintance, ma'am, and to offer my heartfelt apologies for the unacceptable behaviour of my kinsman.'

Melissa's arm muscles contracted, but she was nonetheless able to carry the spoon to her lips. She felt rather than observed Donal's scrutiny. *He knows what it is like to have to manage without a limb, and I am so much more fortunate that my disability is temporary.* She swallowed the porridge and cast an appraising glance at Mr Gunn. His features were set into a calm mask, but she believed his apology to be sincere.

'There is little you can do when a person like George appears on the family tree,' she said carefully. 'I cannot think that you are in any way responsible for his oddness.'

'No. As you say, none of the family is responsible for that. What we might take responsibility for is in not doing sufficient to make your late husband's lawyers understand how dangerous, and possibly mad, the young man is.' Uncle John delivered his speech and sank onto his chair once more. He was elderly and not, Melissa felt, very robust.

'As to that, sir, Harry has made it clear to me that you wrote to Mr Withershaws and received a less than gracious response. I think you have done what you can,' she said, and smiled as widely as she was able. Her skin was still drawn and inflexible around the right side of her mouth, but the muscles on the left allowed her to tease the gentleman a little. She saw the tiny blush that infused his neck before it faded.

'You are too gracious, Lady Pateley. But indeed, Mr Withershaws was not at all. Harry tells me George has arrived in Edinburgh.'

Mrs Gunn protested sharply, but Uncle John merely shrugged. Melissa set her spoon down and drank a little coffee. Here was the cause of the earlier arguments, then. George was around in this bustling city, with its pends and back courts, where a man could hole up and never be found if he did not want to be found. It chilled her.

'Yes, George is in Edinburgh. That is why my nephew allowed your footmen to escort you ladies yesterday evening. He and Zed shadowed your shadow.' Uncle John took a steadying breath. 'It is time we handed you back to your own relatives, Lady Pateley. I hope the letter you received this morning contains an amenable answer from your aunt.'

Melissa choked on her coffee and gurgled. Could anything be less attractive? she thought. It wasn't easy to conjure a riposte when Mr Gunn made such an open attack.

'We aren't spying on you, ma'am, but I happened to arrive at the front door at the same moment as the mail.' While the words were conciliatory, they reminded Melissa of how hard it was to learn all the unspoken foibles of a household. Of course she could not keep her mail secret. However, she had not yet read the letter, and could reply honestly at present while she waited to think of a next step.

'Why she *has* replied, sir; but as I did not want to keep the household waiting, I have not read her letter. It may be that she is from home. I have explained to Harry and Lottie how much the wider family relies on her for assistance in all manner of things.'

'Indeed, that is understandable. I find my own establishment attracts the young as wasps beneath a fruit net.

However, when you have had the opportunity to read the letter, we should be apprised of your prospects without delay.' Uncle John threw back the dregs of his coffee and stood up. Melissa wondered what had tempted her to think he was in any way feeble, and regarded his open features warily.

'Of course, sir. It was always my intention to remove my person from Harry's house as early as possible. I suspect, too, how very dearly Mrs Duart wishes to return to her mama's roof.' Melissa set her cup down with a snap. It was becoming difficult to remember who wanted whom to be staying where and why. She needed to keep her mind focused on her end wish. Harry Gunn was her desire, and she could hardly forward her suit effectively from Newcastle.

'Does she? I have not thought so,' Uncle John said tartly, and sent a questioning glance towards Mrs Gunn. 'Is it true, Henny? Lottie is fretting to be back with you and Harry while

Duart is in Siam?'

'Duart is not in Siam. I had mail this morning also. Duart was blown back by an unseasonable storm and his ship is lying off Plymouth. He says he may abort this mission, as seasickness has afflicted him and his two assistants so badly that they are ill.' Mrs Gunn waved a hand over the pile of letters and cards beside her setting. 'I suppose he will have written this to Lottie also.'

If Uncle John realised she was not answering his question — and Melissa could see from the crease scoring his forehead that he did — he said nothing about it. The Gunn men were formidably intelligent. Had Harry learned his skills through being exposed to them? she wondered. Or maybe the intelligence could also have come from his mama. Lottie was formidable, too.

'Well,' Uncle John said finally, 'whatever Duart decides, Lady Pateley needs to be with the men of her own family.'

'Why do you say this with such firmness, sir?' Melissa was moved to ask. She heard something worrying in Uncle John's voice. It was a hesitation that he did not want to acknowledge, she was sure.

'You are very quick, ma'am.' The old man's veined hands stroked the front of his waistcoat and his fingers dipped into his watch pocket. 'I know we have acted outside the law in snatching you from your house. That house is in England, and it would take the various law officers some time to sort out their jurisdictions, but they would reasonably conclude Harry acted without any lawful orders.' He stepped away from the board. 'It has come to my ears that George intends to lay a complaint against Harry.'

'But I do not intend to lay a complaint against Colonel Gunn,' Melissa protested, although she suspected what was worrying Uncle John.

'I am glad, ma'am. But in the absence of males of your own blood, George has taken it upon himself to send a formal complaint to Mr

Withershaws.' Melissa chilled. 'The lawyer may well approach the present Earl of Pateley as head of your late husband's family; and to put it bluntly, Harry would find himself in difficulties.'

★   ★   ★

Upstairs alone in her room, Melissa broke the seal on the letter from her aunt. She cast an eye over the first paragraphs with their conventional greetings and alternating bits of family news. Halfway down the page, her aunt addressed the request for help in her current predicament.

My Dear Niece, how can you think we would leave you at the mercy of this villain George Gunn and his disordered mind? Your cousins are filled with horror over his antics, which we have now heard more of. I will tell you of that when I see you in person, lest this letter should go astray. Brandon is entirely at your disposal and asks only you allow him to detour to Berwick Old Abbey, where he believes he left some manuscripts when he visited three weeks ago. It is my belief we should all be very grateful to the Lord for designing all body parts to be attached, otherwise Brandon would likely return from visits without his head or some other necessity.

You may lodge with us as long as it is necessary. We must have a family conclave to decide on how we may best proceed. Your uncle Alun was informed this morning by the Withershaws man that he would be making payments to several of the firm's pensioners in Manchester and Newcastle. We are waiting confirmation. There was no clue about why he had this change of heart. Perhaps your Colonel Gunn was able to exert pressure such as we have not found.

On an unrelated subject, I was

intrigued to discover that Colonel Gunn's estate is in Auchenwylde. Your papa had rackety cousins whose family house was in a valley somewhere near Lake Windermere, but were often from home. Indeed, Randolph Flaxxe had been travelling in Scotland around the time of my marriage. He took ship from a port in the north and was never heard of again. Perhaps the same could be arranged for this George Gunn person.

Melissa straightened in her chair and smoothed the crinkling sheets across several times. Rackety cousins. All families had rackety cousins. Why did the mention of Randolph Flaxxe cause the hairs to shiver over her nape? She'd never met him. Why would he travel to Auchenwylde?

Berating herself for fanciful megrims, she folded her aunt's letter and put it away.

13

Melissa rose in anticipation of a visitor. Simmerton had brought Agnes Paxton's card, and in the absence of any of the family, she had asked to have the lady shown upstairs. Sunlight blazed through the huge windows that fronted the square, and she had been sitting in quiet contemplation of dust motes. They hung suspended in still air and danced in the tiny breezes caused when doors opened and closed around the house.

'Lady Pateley, I find you alone, and perhaps resting?' Agnes bustled into the room, shooing Simmerton out again as if she had the right. Melissa damped down a tiny smile. Poor Simmerton. She fully expected him to seek retirement in favour of Percy as soon as it became possible to find him a cottage and pension.

'My dear ma'am, I will retreat immediately if that scowl is my responsibility,' Agnes protested, and Melissa gathered her scattered wits.

'I do beg your pardon, Mrs Paxton. I was momentarily distracted by an unpleasant thought.' It was no more than the truth, but she was not about to reveal her family's fight with Withershaws to such a new friend.

'Agnes. Please call me Agnes. I save Mrs Paxton for only those who need to be reminded of Thomas's rank.' The lady crossed to the windows and gazed out onto the gardens. 'I do believe Thomas and Harry . . . ' She took a deep breath. ' . . . and that scamp Zed are enjoying all the skulduggery. There are five pensioned-off soldiers in various states of decay cluttering the gardens this morning. It would not surprise me at all if Edinburgh's police are called to deal with them.'

Melissa giggled. 'Why, ma'am, I cannot think what prompts you to describe Zed as a scamp. Joanie and I are still daunted by his scowl.'

'Joanie?' Agnes queried gently. 'I wonder.'

Melissa watched her tiny visitor's back, ramrod straight and carrying a head at full alert. What exactly was the colonel's wife looking at with such interest?

As if sensing the change in her hostess, Agnes chose that moment to turn back into the room. Melissa was forced to attend to her comfort.

'I hope you are able to stay for a visit, Agnes. Mrs Gunn and Lottie have walked out to Uncle John's house, I believe.' She watched her visitor take a seat and then sat down herself. 'You mention skulduggery?'

'I suppose I should not,' Agnes said, and sighed deeply. 'However, I cannot be doing with it. Thomas is older than me by some ten years, and it is a gap which enables him to pontificate. He would have our children believe I am incapable of adding up a household balance sheet on occasion.'

Melissa laughed aloud. The very idea was ridiculous. Mrs Paxton's beautiful country house ran on oiled wheels that no featherbrain could have achieved. She was relieved to see her visitor smile broadly.

'It is an amazing trial we women have to put up with. My papa, however, was ahead of his time, and I was always allowed access to his thoughts. It enabled me to take over the running of much of his business in due course.'

'Your husband?'

'Neville truly could not read sheets of figures, and he was always glad to hear my thoughts before he set off for meetings with our lawyers.' Melissa sighed. She was in serious danger of forgetting her earlier decision and brought the conversation back. 'However, these are melancholy thoughts. What is the skulduggery you think of? It sounds more exciting than repining on female disenfranchisement.'

'Ah, yes. Thomas, Harry and Zed had discovered that George Gunn had been seen by one of Harry's ex-soldiers crossing the roadway around the Causewayside Tollhouse.' Agnes straightened her shoulders and fingered the delicate silver necklace lying in her throat. 'They were not playing cards last night. They were outside watching shadows.'

'And finding substance,' Melissa added. 'Uncle John came early to tell Mrs Gunn, and he also told me.'

'Good. I was anxious lest you thought to hold it against Harry's character when he did not escort you home.' Agnes pulled up her reticule and dropped her gaze while she fiddled with its strings.

Melissa narrowed her good eye in consternation. What murmurings had reached the ears of this elegant friend of Harry's? She also squared her shoulders and would have challenged Agnes to explain her remark, but the door opened and the object of their discussion strode into the room.

'Agnes,' Harry said, and Melissa

heard a shade of defensiveness in his tone. 'Thomas thought you might have been making a call on my mama.'

'Your mama has gone off to Mr John Gunn's house with Lottie,' Agnes replied. Melissa saw how she now kept her gaze fixed on the floor as if the Turkish rugs held some universal secret. 'I hoped to further my acquaintance with Lady Pateley. It is not possible to talk of serious matters when one's drawing room is full of casual visitors.'

'Serious matters?' Harry queried, and Melissa began to suspect she was in a different plane while these two old friends exchanged pleasantries that were as barbed as any satire by Mr Sheridan. 'Surely you understand Lady Pateley will be with us only for a matter of days, now that her cousin posts from Newcastle to bring her home?'

'He does?' The words escaped Melissa, but in truth she was astonished. No arrangements were finally in place, and her cousin

Brandon was notorious for meandering. His mama had reminded her of it when she wrote. She might just as well have held her peace. The others continued their discussion as if she had not spoken.

'Come now, Gunn. Is there any certainty as to the probable date of Lady Pateley's departure?' Agnes said with spirit. Melissa would have admired her for it had she been discussing her own business rather than Melissa's. As it was, she saw colour surge up Harry's neck and suffuse the beard growing around his chin. Had he had no time to shave that morning? she wondered.

'Agnes, please. Do not add to our difficulties. While it will be, would have been . . . ' Harry spluttered to a halt, but gathered his thoughts with a sweep of a huge hand across his forehead and continued. 'It may be that we will be able to entertain Lady Pateley and her relatives in the future, possibly after she has married. But at the moment, various exigencies — I mean . . . '

'I know what exigencies are, Harry Gunn! What is not clear to you mutton-headed males is what is under your noses.' Agnes rose and strode around the rugs. She slapped a hand against her thigh as if she were urging on her horse. Melissa waited in fascination. 'George Gunn.'

Melissa held her breath and let the words drip ice into her heart. What could Agnes mean by this theatrical explosion?

'Thomas promised . . . '

'And he kept his promise,' Agnes interrupted the ashen-faced Harry. 'Only you gentlemen speak so loudly when excited, and Thomas does not always remember that an ancient mansion house such as ours in Charles Street will hold fewer secrets than a modern one with close-fitting doors.'

Melissa understood then. Harry had shared the supposed secret of his birth with Thomas, but Agnes had overheard all. No wonder the lady had been so circumspect last evening. No wonder

Uncle John wanted her shipped out of the capital and delivered into her birth family's care. These things seeped into the common knowledge with such heart-stopping ease.

'George Gunn is a man who preys on others,' Harry said.

'He may be,' Agnes agreed. 'But he may be a pawn.'

'You're speaking in riddles, Agnes. In what sense might George be a pawn?'

'Why, he might be a way of some other man getting close to the countess. A man whose position does not allow him to sneak around or climb up ivy-clad walls.' A cold sensation crawled up Melissa's spine.

'You mean David Withershaws,' she uttered. 'You think he controls George and uses him like a puppet?'

'I don't know of anyone called Withershaws. In fact, I do not have any person in mind. What prompts me to speak is the way George Gunn attacks and then retreats instantly. It's almost as if he performs a set task, and then . . . ' Agnes paced a little more while she was clearly ordering her thoughts. 'When he has performed his task and it has gone wrong, as it so often seems to do, he withdraws in order to take fresh instruction.'

★　★　★

Harry curled his hands into fists and dug his nails into the palms. Anything to stop the scream of frustration rising in his throat. He held Agnes Paxton's reluctant gaze and bore into her as if his stare could elicit answers. Why had she listened in? Surely no gently born person would keep silent after realising they were party to such a sensitive discussion as the one he'd had with Thomas.

'I know you hold me accountable, Gunn, and I do not blame you,' she muttered, inflaming the anger swelling in his chest.

'Agnes, perhaps it would be best if

you left now,' Melissa said. He watched how she softened her request with a shy smile. 'Harry and I have had so little time to discuss events, and I fear his mama and sister will return before we are able to cover as much ground as I would wish.'

Harry loosened his fingers. The countess chose her words with great care and did not speak for him. Was the relief that flooded him the kind of reaction no woman ever experienced because their menfolk prosed on about how they must or should feel or react? He took a deep breath. Neville Pateley had been a lucky man; Neville Pateley had possibly no understanding of exactly how lucky he had been. He, on the other hand, knew he would never enjoy this woman's caring partnership.

'We have little to discuss, ma'am,' he snapped.

'Is that so, sir? Why, my aunt's letter made much of Brandon detouring to Berwick Old Abbey, and yet you tell

Agnes he is posting straight to Edinburgh. May we not begin a discussion there?'

Damn! Harry thought. *How can I admire her intelligence and wit and then expect her to turn it all to sleep when I must have my will prevail?*

'I don't know what your aunt wrote, Lady Pateley, but I took the direction from the outside of your letter and have sent Mr Flaxxe clear instructions.'

'I see. You think to influence my cousin's attitude to travel and to the calendar?' She sat on, but Harry saw the tension across her shoulders and ached with the wish to massage them as Zed had shown him. The thought made his reply brusquer than it needed to be. He knew as soon as the words tumbled from his mouth he should have moderated them.

'I know how to send an order that will not be misconstrued.'

'Of course. That military slant.'

Melissa took a breath, and he hoped it steadied her. But at the same time, he so wished she would faint and then he would catch her, it squeezed the breath from his chest and he had to remind himself to breathe again.

'My cousin may appreciate the turn of phrase, Harry, but I assure you it will not influence his timetable one jot. He has apparently left a manuscript in the Old Abbey . . . '

'Then which of your cousins does understand need and urgency? Why have we put our reliance on one who has his head in the clouds?' Harry shouted, goaded by exasperation. A thought was forming in his brain, and he did not like it one iota. 'Agnes, perhaps you would leave us, please.'

They all hesitated. Agnes clearly did not like being ordered, but he knew she would never stay on in his house after he had expressly asked her to leave it. Melissa was flushing up the left side of her neck and over her face. He even wondered if a tiny blush was shining through the skin over her right cheek. On another occasion, he would have so enjoyed exploring that possibility of returning life, but today he had other concerns.

He closed the door behind Agnes and turned toward his remaining guest. 'Now, ma'am, please explain the puzzle to me.'

'Puzzle?'

Oh Melissa, he thought, and closed his eyes over the myriad whys and wherefores that remained between them and a happy resolution of this affair.

'Why, when you have six adult male cousins, have you asked for escort from one who pays so little heed to urgency and timetables that he might, just might, ignore an instruction from me?'

He distanced himself in case he should reach for her and drag her into his arms to remind her of the spark flaring between them. Worse, he remembered the many times he'd tumbled Kitty and Mairie over his thighs and beat a tattoo on their wriggling behinds. Like an older brother might in the absence of any proper authority from a parent. Like a husband might when pushed beyond exasperation by a wife unconscious of her own safety.

'Is that a puzzle to you, Harry?'

He returned in a single stride and hauled her from her chair. With a groan of mingled frustration and loathing, he brought his head down and kissed her as she so deserved to be kissed.

Melissa held tightly to Harry's shoulders as her light shawl slipped toward the floor. She revelled in the power of the man. His arms secured her and his mouth ravished hers with a fire of longing she returned full measure. It was so long since she'd enjoyed the pleasures of an adult relationship, so very long. Harry must know they were suited. In his heart, he must know.

The deepening fervour of his kiss was a balm after the months of fear and pain she'd endured. He did not spare her, but gathered her buttocks in his hands, wonderful hands that had cared for her and eased the discomfort of her injuries, and lifted her from her feet against the hard planes of his thighs. Her body moulded with his, and the precious moments slid from them until he lifted his head away and gazed down into her very soul.

Melissa let out a tiny startled sigh of distress. Why was he so angry, so full of — hate, almost? Surely Harry could not hate her?

'You must leave here, Melissa, before we dishonour everything any decent folk hold dear.'

So, no knowledge in his heart, she thought as cooling air swirled from an open window. *He simply cannot control himself.*

He set her apart, and went to stand gazing out onto the gardens while she adjusted her clothing and lifted her shawl from the floor. How dare he accuse her?

'You must give up on me, Lady Pateley. You must go to Newcastle where your relatives will be able to advise you — and this time . . . ' He breathed deeply and hard. The noise was distressing, but she could see he was determined to say everything he was feeling. 'This time, you must follow their advice. You must marry the man they think will bring you not only happiness, but honour.'

'You make yourself very clear, Colonel Gunn. Perhaps while I await my relative's arrival, you would move to your uncle's house?'

'No, I will move to Thomas's house and ask my mama to invite him and Agnes to stay here. Now that she has settled this canker about George being manipulated into your brain, I do not expect Agnes to create any more mischief. I may mention the matter to Thomas.'

Melissa did not watch Harry's rigidly staid departure, but she felt the floor tremble through every stride. *I would not lay odds on Agnes paying much attention to her lord,* she thought. *Perhaps all is not lost yet.*

Withershaws. How everything comes back to that man!

Melissa mused over the idea. It was not as far-fetched as Harry thought. He had not experienced Withershaws' lustful gaze or his cleverly wandering hands that grasped one above one's waist. He had no knowledge of the man's obsessive longing for an entrée into the haut ton.

I do.

14

Amidst the bustle of the Lawnmarket, Harry huddled against the flank of his horse. He was able to keep an eye on Zed's straight back. The other man stood with a peddler. Coins jingled, and a strip of ribbon was torn from a reel in exchange. Zed wrapped it in a clean handkerchief and, as Harry watched, stuffed the impromptu parcel into his coat pocket.

The mouths of all the pends were busy with folk, and Harry was alert for a sighting of George Gunn's tall figure. Riddle's Court and Fisher's Close disgorged natives and visitors alike. A sedan chair stopped and Lady Grizelda Stuart emerged. One of her servants had been posted to watch for her arrival and stepped forward to pay the chairmen. He turned back to assist Lady Stuart across the rubbish-strewn flags, and in that second, Harry saw his quarry.

Zed did, too, and turned with an arm raised in their agreed signal before he walked off the steps onto the bed of the road and crossed towards Lady Stair's close. Harry knew he would be following George. He tugged Gorse's bridle. The gelding's bulk enabled him to walk upright, but he hoped the horse didn't spook over anything and dip and buck too much. Rats and cats vied with the many loitering dogs over scraps of bone and other matter. Harry watched as a tiny child threw a stone and disturbed a gaggle of squabbling cats. His stomach recoiled when the child bent to haul a huge piece of fish from their midst and ran off cackling in triumph.

'I do hope his mother turns that away.'

Harry's head snapped round, and his gaze locked with Melissa's. She had alighted from a sedan chair, and Percy was paying off the men. Harry sent the young footman a scowl of frustration and anger. Had he not instructed all the servants, his and Melissa's, that she was not to be allowed to leave George Square? The younger man blushed, but could say nothing at present.

'Lady Pateley.'

'Harry.'

'I have some business that needs my urgent attention, ma'am. I hope you will accept my apologies and have Percy call another chair to return you to the comparative safety of George Square.'

'I think not, sir. I had no expectation of meeting with you when I set off. Your occupation does not inconvenience me.' She spoke the words lightly, but Harry knew he'd alerted her. She allowed her gaze to sweep around the crowds and only slowly brought it back to his face. 'It must be hard to ride through such a press.'

'Gorse is used to the crowds. He needs a certain amount of exercise, and I would usually take him for a canter around the Boroughloch. This morning, however, I was unable to do that.' It was lame. Harry knew he'd lost sight of Zed by now, and the possibility that George had doubled back from the court he'd gone into was searing his brain. There were one or two of his men around in the area besides Zed, and he would have to rely on their capabilities.

'Does Mr George Gunn wander this area?'

'Melissa! I gave instructions that you were not to leave George Square . . . '

'Indeed, but I pay Percy's wages. It is unfortunate that you have driven a wedge between me and my men. I did not enjoy reminding him, and he did not enjoy being reminded. Servants do best, sir, under one master.'

Harry bowed imperceptibly. As so often since he realised Melissa could never be his, anger filled his breast. She simply refused to see it. She wanted to carry on as if the secret of his birth would never become public knowledge. Melissa's next remark caught him unawares.

'Yet again, I ask a question and you distract me in order to avoid an answer.'

'He does,' Harry said, dragging his overtaxed brain into the here and now. 'Yes, George Gunn is wandering these courts, and I can only trust Zed has him still in his view.'

'Because I have caused you to lose your concentration. I am sorry, Harry. It was not my intention. I came out to visit my banker's representatives.' Melissa raised a hand to adjust the set of her hat. Joanie had secured it over her wig, but the wind was strong as it blasted through the open close from the mound. 'If you wish, I will walk back to the square now.'

'That's not far, but far enough for someone recovering their strength. We should whistle up another chair,' Harry said. Could she safely walk back, he wondered. George might be anywhere by now. He would have to accompany her. There was no chance that Percy was carrying a weapon, and every chance that George had armed himself with anything sharp that could be concealed about his person.

'I must return with you. Percy, fall in. Take the horse, if you will.'

* * *

Melissa set her fingers on the arm Harry proffered and ignored the inner voice berating her for making such a foolish jaunt. The months of invalidism had prompted it, she knew. There was no sense of bravado in defying Harry's instructions. He would not believe that, of course, but she knew. She simply could not pass another day without exerting herself over her affairs. That was the reason for her foray.

'I was enclosed in the chair,' she said with more diffidence than she liked to hear. 'Hidden from the gaze of passers-by — whether they were friend or foe.'

'So you were, ma'am. And Percy?'

His dry tone alerted her to the knowledge that she was not yet restored to her full faculties of reasoning. George certainly knew who Percy was. As the young man had been chosen in the first place for his imposing height and pleasing appearance, he was going to be visible among the crowds of folk on the streets.

'Ah, yes. Harry, why are you afraid the secret of your parentage will be revealed now?' She had learned a few tricks in the several days she'd known Harry Gunn, and sprung the question as she'd witnessed him do with others.

'Take care there,' he said as he guided her around a toppled pile of cloth. 'Melissa, my sister is very conscious of her status.' They walked on towards the junction where the road disappeared down into the Grassmarket below the shadow of Edinburgh's great castle. Harry was silent as if he'd said more than he intended.

'I can understand that. She fell from grace. It is a difficult thing to stay vigilant and not give away any inklings of past secrets, but she has done so well,' Melissa agreed. Perhaps Harry was going to share a little honest information with her. Chill settled in her neck, and she gripped his sleeve so hard that she felt his gaze sweep her face in reaction. Did she want honest information? she wondered.

'You begin to see the problem, then. Vigilance is all very well, but family likenesses seep out; and perhaps as I grow older, my bone structure will lead persons to question my parentage.' A broken basket stuffed with noxious matter flew through the air from the toe of Harry's boot.

'You think that?' Melissa was overcome. 'I wonder what would spur such thoughts? Perhaps your sister is not as ingratiating as she might be, and Mrs Duart, her mama-in-law, might seek revenge for an injury?'

'Perhaps; but my reasoning tells me that Mistress Duart has kept the secret this long and will take it to her grave. It would make her look self-seeking to reveal it now when her eldest grandson is approaching the time he might begin to look for a bride.' Harry stopped talking again; and again, Melissa was filled with frustration. 'On the other hand, that eldest grandson, born of a registered marriage, is the legitimate heir.'

Ahead of them the crowds banked up around a toppled cart. Horses reared then fell back in the press of vehicles and she wondered whether any were hurt. Harry glanced back at his precious gelding, but he also looked everywhere and she knew again that she had behaved badly in making this expedition. If Harry Gunn was nervous, then perhaps she should be, too.

'No, it is not those who have kept the secret, Melissa. It is those who now want other things. Those who want you.'

'Me? You mean George,' she exclaimed. 'We know the man is mad, and no one would give credence to his ramblings.'

'It is not only — '

'Colonel,' Percy shouted from behind

them. Melissa glanced up and caught sight of Harry's large horse bolting. The crowd parted to allow the panicked animal to pass, and Melissa briefly saw a dart protruding from its flank. *That was deliberate*, she thought. *Who did that?* The crowd came back together, shouting and gesticulating as the horse ploughed on through the press.

'Follow him, Percy,' Harry called. For a few seconds his arm dropped, and Melissa had to steady herself as the ground became uneven. It was long enough for someone to lift her from her feet and toss her unceremoniously onto the tail of a cart. She squirmed as best she could, trying to get onto her knees, but a huge blanket covered her form, and then weight pinned her legs. It was heavy, but flexible. Another person, she thought as the cart moved slowly into the throng.

Has anyone seen this outrage? Where is Harry?

⋆　⋆　⋆

The cart did not travel far before it lurched over rough ground and stopped. The jolting shook every one of her bones, and Melissa was hard put not to scream. She *would* not scream, lest her captors thought she was afraid of them. She might be afraid, but she was also angry. These people had abducted her violently and, it tore at her heartstrings and disrupted her chance to learn more about Harry Gunn. She hated them.

The weight slid from her legs, and she heard a dull thud as it landed on soft ground. Were they on the edge of one of the city's many building sites, or even in the shrubby wasteland that was the Boroughloch? It was difficult to catch any smell beneath the thick blanket, but she detected malt.

'Fool! Take better care with the lady. She is not to be injured.'

Melissa's heart stopped. George Gunn. She knew his voice. Her limbs trembled as blood thumped through them again. The blanket was pulled and then eased off her shoulders. She clutched her reticule as if her life depended on its retention, and groaned when she realised her hat and wig were askew.

George Gunn. What idiocy did the man think he was about now? Zed and his gaggle of soldiers would be around and about like a pack of hounds loosed after the fox.

Light streamed as the coarse material was stripped away, and George himself assisted her off the tail of the cart. She heard oxen snorting and knew that if they had pulled the cart, it could not have come far at all from the point these men lifted her. They were several, and they were dressed in workaday clothes with handkerchiefs around their faces and shapeless hats pulled down about their ears. Probably also former soldiers, but less disciplined than Harry's men. They glowered at George, and she sensed his shouted orders did not suit their idea of their own status. She would remember that.

'Harry!' she squealed as she saw him supine on the ground. The weight across her legs had been his. 'What have you done, George Gunn? I'll see you transported for this.'

'Calmly, Melissa.'

'Calmly! How dare you! How dare you commit this outrage? Colonel Gunn's men will be after you and these fellows.' She clasped the bed of the cart to steady herself and was dismayed by how weak she felt. Screaming at George would achieve nothing, she berated herself inwardly. If ever there was a need for clear reasoned thinking, this was the moment.

'Really?' George motioned to one of the men, and she felt a hand slide around her waist. In other circumstances, she would be grateful for such support, but at present it simply inflamed her temper.

'Tell this brute to unhand me, sir.'

'Allow Lady Pateley to test her balance.'

The man heard that and pulled his

arm roughly back, sending Melissa against the cart. She thrust her left hand out and managed to stop herself falling to the ground. At her feet she caught an infinitesimal movement of Harry's leg. She groaned dramatically. George was instantly solicitous and diverted from anything Harry might be able to achieve.

'Are you hurt, Melissa?' The concern oozed from George's words, and although she was no longer fooled, she determined to use it to her advantage. Would it not, she thought, be a good thing to drive a wedge between the man and his helpers?

'Besides the bruising I must have sustained when these oafs threw me onto a dung cart. What do you believe, sir?' She let go of the cart and shifted a little towards Harry's motionless form. Another foot and she would be able to touch his thigh and feel whether he gathered his muscles for a leap from the ground.

'It's no a dung cart, wumman,' one of

the men exclaimed. 'Dae ye think we're daft? Catch the plague or something worse from one o they. Naw, this is a brewer's dray.'

'Loquacious,' Melissa said, and wondered if Harry's shoulders twitched. She needed to be careful. They hadn't thought to tie either of their wrists, and there was far less possibility of escaping if Harry was bound.

George sighed. 'Too many words, my lady, and we waste time. The carriage, Crowdie, while I deal with this great pudding.'

Melissa heard tack jangling from a vehicle behind her. She could not see it. George drew a dagger out of the top of his boot just as rough hands gripped her above her elbows and a knee hit the backs of her thighs so she fell against the devil behind her. This was the moment to scream. Off-balance and surrounded, there was nothing her personal strength would achieve. She could not even pull a pin from her drooping hat, but if the fellow once slipped his hold, she would.

Gathering a lungful of air, she let out a screech that would have rivalled anything uttered by Macbeth's witches, and another before the brute let go her left arm and brought his hand over her mouth. It was enough room to play, and she knew she must act now, or George would kill Harry as he lay winded on the street.

The hat-pin snagged but came free; and using every last bit of her draining strength, Melissa stuck it back and up into the neck of the man who held her. His blood spurted hot and sticky over her and he released her abruptly. She stumbled, but another man caught her. When she would have stabbed him, too, Zed's voice stopped her.

'He's one of us, Lady Pateley. He's one of us.' Melissa slumped against the man, but was soon on her feet and watching with concern as Zed ministered to Harry.

'There's so much blood,' she whispered to no one in particular.

'Aye, an' your ladyship was responsible for a wheen o' it,' the man who'd pried her away from George's villainous helper said and laughed. Melissa would have joined in, but she needed to see Harry open his eyes. Surely George hadn't managed to plunge his blade into an artery before Zed and his fellows turned up?

'Leslie,' Zed snapped without turning, 'give me your arm here.' Together, the two able-bodied men of the group shifted Harry's weight and got him into a sitting position. His head lolled before coming to rest on one huge shoulder, and Melissa could wait no longer. She dropped to his side and grabbed hold of his face in both hands.

'Harry, Harry. Say something.'

'I might if you weren't cutting off my circulation.' The voice was slow, and if she hadn't known better, she might have thought the words were slurred, but they were Harry's. She leant back on her thighs and was helped upright by Zed.

'Your ladyship needs to let the maister breathe. He's had worse.'

'Tha' dunt he got at . . .'

'Thank you, Leslie. Her ladyship doesn't need to hear about our exploits on the peninsula.' Zed spoke with his usual calm, but Melissa knew there was a warning there, too. She stepped sideways to allow the men to ease Harry onto his feet.

What made me think the two of us were going to escape? George's crew are ruthless.

'I think I can stand,' Harry said at last. The men released their hold and he took a few small tentative steps. 'Thank the Lord you managed to follow.'

'Indeed.' Zed was sending glances all around, and Melissa caught sight of a small commotion towards the main road. Several of Harry's men were hustling a prisoner through the gathering crowd. She saw Percy skirt the fracas and lead Gorse into view. The great horse hung its head as if it realised the part its bolting had played in her abduction. Together, man and beast paced along.

'Do you ride?' Zed asked the footman.

'Yes, sir.' Percy stared at Harry's drooping form. The young man was pale, but under Zed's scrutiny, he lifted his shoulders back and attended. 'Would you like me to take Lady Pateley back to George Square?'

'I think it's for the best. Here, give me the bridle.' Zed held the horse while Percy stepped up onto the tail of the cart and manoeuvred a foot into one of the stirrups. As Gorse took his weight, he backed a bit and threw his head. The tack jangled, but Percy brought him under control and held him steady.

'Now, ma'am,' Zed said, and Melissa came forward meekly. This was not the moment to indulge in hysterics, she knew. Within a minute she was on the horse in front of her manservant, and they moved off. She saw men wearing the suits of Harry's household keeping pace with them through the crowds.

There was little chance of George succeeding in a second attempt.

15

As they approached the square, Melissa wondered what explanation she might give for her total dishevelment. Percy must have wondered, too, because she felt the horse slow to a walk. They veered into the service lane and crossed the square at its southern end.

'This way,' a rough voice called. 'Simmerton and Miss Joanie are in the basement area.' After a heartbeat of hesitation, Percy decided to go with the instruction and brought Gorse calmly to the railings behind the Gunn house. Joanie and Simmerton were up the outside stair in a flash and assisted Melissa to slide down from the horse. Within a minute, she was down the stairs and through the door into the servants' passage. It clanged shut behind her.

Almost three hours passed in a blur

of mental turmoil Melissa could hardly remember ever having experienced. Even the days after Neville's death had not demanded as much from her. She chewed the nails on her left hand and snapped at Joanie, Simmerton and Percy, who dared to return from the stables without news of either Harry or George Gunn.

There was a sharp rap on her door, and Harry entered. Joanie dropped a deep curtsey and scuttled from the room. Melissa glanced up and caught her tongue between her teeth to prevent the cry that would have escaped. Harry was bruised around his left eye where the villains must have clubbed him and knocked him out as he stood with her on the roadway.

He swayed a little and sat down unceremoniously in a chair. Melissa took a step towards him, but changed her mind and settled onto a sofa.

'Harry, I am truly sorry my thoughtless behaviour has led to this.'

'Calmly, ma'am. George's plans were

well advanced before your appearance in the Lawnmarket. I suspect that actually foiled his attempt, because I had so many men shadowing him while he was in public areas and we were well placed to intervene.' He stretched his legs in front of him and sighed. 'It does not do to make plans and then change them without thought.'

'Surely spontaneity has its place?' she protested.

'Surely it does, but only when it has been weighed and found to be a better plan than the one being discarded. George's men are rough. They are ill-disciplined and interested only in his brass. They are unlikely to move as a team in the way that Zed has our men drilled.'

She thought about this and mentally conceded its truth. George had possibly tried to abduct her in such a busy place simply because he saw her suddenly before his eyes. His plan might have been to lift her from a less crowded street out of sight of anyone but Percy.

She shuddered. Percy might have paid a high price in such circumstances.

'You may be correct.'

'Why, and it is very good of you to find something I may lay claim to, Lady Pateley.'

Melissa bristled over his tone. 'I do not claim any knowledge of military strategy, sir. There's no need for you to fly into the boughs as if I were trying to usurp your position as commander-in-chief of the George Square Soap soldiers.'

His laugh bellowed in the empty Edinburgh drawing room, and Melissa concealed the smile that tugged at her lips. She was glad to have made him laugh and not pursue his imagined grudge. Perhaps Lottie was wont to interfere too much in his life and he feared she was following the example?

'I have passed an unhappy afternoon worrying about you, and now I see there was no need. Your head is clearly as thick as if it were carved from wood.'

'Hmn! What wood do you allow me?

A dark and handsome teak, perhaps, or . . .'

'Enough! I think you hold yourself in such high esteem I do not need to search for hardwoods of regal tendencies. Besides, we may ask Mr Duart when he finally arrives from the south.' Melissa straightened her skirts. She had been washed and changed by a Joanie she hardly recognised. A Joanie who almost dared to tell her off for being such a fool and who would not smile until Harry's step was heard on the flags of the hall downstairs. She straightened her skirts, but what she wanted to straighten was the mass of blond hair curling over Harry's brow. She felt his eyes on her.

'Something trouble you, ma'am?'

'Beyond the mess of my life, do you mean?'

'It holds a considerable degree of interest, I must agree. George, it seems, has pressed Withershaws into action.' His light tone did not fool Melissa for a second. This was news to support

Uncle John's request that she go south as soon as possible.

'Your uncle was afraid of something of this nature. I am more sanguine, however, as Mr Withershaws does not hold the family's regard in the way he once did.'

'I know you believe that, but he is a slippery eel, David Withershaws. My main hope in this debacle is that he and George will cancel each other.' Harry wriggled again. 'However, I have no wish to find myself thrown into any holding cell while the lawyers argue over whether I abducted you or not.'

'George abducted me,' Melissa countered furiously. 'It is becoming something of an open sport.'

'Ma'am, I do beg your pardon for the discomfort and anxiety, although I might point out that the sparkle back in your eyes belies the weight of either.'

'I protest . . . '

'Of course, but I do not absolutely believe you. Melissa. I must leave the city for a few days. Thomas and Zed will look to your protection meantime, and when your cousin finally arrives, they will bolster the effect of his name with men.' He stood, and Melissa rose, too, in some consternation.

'Leave the city?' A black hole of anxiety opened in her mind.

'There is no choice. Zed will always find me, and I would come back for you; but it is mostly the case that matters will blow over if the person one was arguing with is no longer available for a fight.'

'The law has a long memory,' she said, and hated the fear tingeing her words.

'And so it should. But when your menfolk show their solidarity, Withershaws will have far less support for the prosecution of a case.'

'I will be resolute, Harry.'

'Melissa, I would ask you a question of a little sensitivity, and I wish that you wait till I have said all before attempting an answer.' His sombre tone and severe expression touched her nerves. She knew how perceptive Harry could be, and wondered whether he had noticed anything in her reactions to Withershaws's name. It was not always as easy as she wished to prevent a shudder throbbing through her.

'Personal questions do not always lead to harmony even among the closest and best of friends, sir,' she replied. She saw the raising of his brows and tightening of his jaw muscles and relented. He would have his information; and if it were something sensitive he needed to know, perhaps it was better for her to provide it, she thought. 'I will listen, though.'

'Why does Withershaws pursue a vendetta against you?' So, it was about Withershaws. When would she be free of the devil?

'He wants my money brought under the control of my oldest surviving uncle, which would be under his own.'

'No, I do not believe it is as simple as that, my dear. He pursues you as the lawyer of the Flaxxe family, and yet his motives are muddled. Does he . . . '

Melissa opened her mouth, but Harry raised his hand and she lapsed into silence. He was the picture of concentration. His hair slipped over his brow and framed the strong face. His body was still and hardly moved as he let his arm drop back onto the chair. She shivered.

I begin to see where he finds confusion here, and of course I do know why.

'What is clear to me, and the lawyers I have consulted, is that Withershaws has no basis in English law for holding onto your family monies. It is also true that he is acting outside the remit of his principal. Your eldest uncle rarely confers with him, and the other family members have made strong representations about his overweening interference in company business.'

I cannot tell him. Shame holds me back, even though I know I hold none of the blame.

'You hesitate.' His eyes betrayed the

disappointment he clearly felt. Why couldn't she entrust her secret to him when they had shared so much and come so far? 'So be it, but this thing will never be resolved until we can nip it at the roots.' Harry stood up with as much speed as his injuries allowed and towered over her. 'I sincerely hope you will think better of this decision, Melissa. I will always listen.'

The tiny bow he made before leaving tore at her heartstrings more than anything else in her life.

David Withershaws is the devil incarnate.

★ ★ ★

The next couple of days dragged by as the women settled into a routine without Harry's central presence. Melissa received a lot of mail, as her aunt had obviously given her direction to her cousins. Making up perhaps for lost time, the ladies wrote and filled their pages with domestic detail about their houses and babies and growing sons. Melissa was glad to hear it all. She took her duties seriously. It was useful to know who was growing up and might be good in the business. Besides, business interested her and diverted her wandering thoughts whenever a giant with blond locks threatened to overwhelm her good sense.

On the morning of the third day following Harry's departure, Melissa was again alone in his George Square house. The rattle sounded up and down, and in the quiet she heard Simmerton's heels snap across the downstairs flags. He had taken it on himself to act as arbiter of who came and went through the front door, and Mrs Gunn appeared to enjoy having a stately English butler greet her friends.

'Of course the countess will see me, you old fool . . . '

Melissa's blood chilled.

'I am the legal representative of her Uncle Walter, and as such must be the most important visitor she could receive.' The nasal twang carried up the stairwell and brought Joanie skittering into the drawing room.

'Find Percy,' Melissa said as calmly as she could, but it was a thread of sound. 'And Matt, and send them here before that man climbs the stairs.'

While Simmerton ushered Withershaws into Mrs Gunn's tiny front room beside the entrance, Melissa gathered her thoughts and her courage. Percy, Matt and Joanie arrived as Simmerton brought Withershaws's card on a tray. She ignored it and gazed around at her 'troops'.

'Whatever he says, you must not leave the room.' Melissa said at last. 'Even if I instruct you to leave the room, you must stay.'

'My lady?' Percy asked. The frown that split his young forehead made her smile ruefully.

'It is a puzzle, Percy, but he has weapons in his speech, and I may forget how important it is that I should not be alone with him.' The men bowed and took up positions. Melissa thought Matt looked disappointed that Withershaws's weapons were verbal ones. She had no doubt he was spoiling for a fight, as he'd missed out on the action with George. Joanie sat towards the back of the room. Simmerton retreated to the ground floor to bring the lawyer up.

'My lady.' Withershaws made the words a parody of politeness. 'I am so glad to see you looking as well as may be in the difficult circumstances you are forced to endure.'

'Endure?' Melissa raised her brows fleetingly. 'Why do use such an unfriendly word, sir, when I am staying here as Mrs Henrietta Gunn's guest?'

'Mrs Gunn is wholly under the influence of her criminal son, Colonel Henry Gunn, and may yet regret her decision to accommodate you. Besides, ma'am, when you are used to the trappings of your station, why would you stay in a hovel such as this?'

Melissa bristled. He was so clever in

his approach, trying to lead her away from the real matters at the heart of his visit by making her defend her friends and their home. She schooled her features into silence and waited.

'I cannot approach the matter of my visit freely in the hearing of your domestics, ma'am. Have you forgotten the niceties of society already?' The lawyer snapped his words without apparently giving much thought to their effect on his listeners. Melissa caught sight of an infinitesimal movement that told her Matt was itching to grab the man by the coat and toss him downstairs. She sympathised. Her own arm itched for a riding crop with which to lay about the villain.

'I do not wish to dismiss my people, Mr Withershaws. If you are unable to state your business in their hearing, then perhaps you would care to put it in writing to Battle and Wharton.' Melissa had thrown down her gauntlet, and watched Withershaws's eyes narrow. He was no doubt reluctant to approach her respectable men of business again, having been bested several times already by their superior expertise.

'Battle and Wharton are very well in their way, Lady Pateley, but their way is slow and cumbersome. When, as now, a lady of my distinguished client's family is held a virtual prisoner . . . '

'Disabuse yourself of this belief, Mr Withershaws. I am here as a guest of Mrs Gunn.'

'Brought here, abducted one may say, by a buffoon who does not know peace has arrived in this land and soldiering is considered archaic, even uncouth,' Withershaws blasted the words at her.

'Abducted?' Melissa smoothed the skirts of her magenta morning gown with her left hand. 'Why, if any abduction is going ahead, you might like to caution your favourite, George Gunn.'

The words wrought a change in the lawyer Melissa had not foreseen. His skin was pock-marked and his complexion pasty, but it fired and paled in an instant. He breathed hard as if something constricted his chest; and had he been any other visitor, Melissa would have asked Percy to offer him assistance. She caught sight of a movement behind Withershaws in the doorway and saw Zed standing there like his absent master would have done, in contemplative silence.

'What can you mean, my lady?' Withershaws brought out in a throaty murmur. 'George Gunn is indeed known to me — but I would not call him a favourite. I have heard how he would make you a decent offer of marriage, but abduction? Surely, ma'am, your wits have been — '

'Turned by exposure to the chill Edinburgh wind?' Melissa asked. 'I think not, sir. I know when I have been tossed onto a brewer's dray and covered by stinking hessian.'

Zed moved with cat-like quiet across the rugs till he stood just behind Withershaws. Melissa could not tell from his expression whether he wished she had kept that information to themselves, but the stiff set of his upper arms and broad shoulders hinted she had spoken out of turn.

'Good morning, my lady,' Zed said, and Withershaws turned to view the newcomer. 'The women told me downstairs you had a visitor from England.'

Withershaws shuffled. Melissa could see how the interview was turning sour for him. No one would underestimate the power emanating from Zed.

'I've had no opportunity to speak to you alone, Lady Pateley, and now here is another intruder in your drawing-room. My client will not be pleased to know you were kept from me in this uncouth manner. I suppose it is Scotland.' Withershaws sought to shift blame and divert her. What was it about George's abduction attempt that exercised him so?

Zed bowed and turned to the irate lawyer. He towered over the man by a head, and Withershaws stepped back, banging his thin calf against the chair he had not managed to sit on.

'Mr Withershaws, I would be pleased to escort you to a sedan chair.'

'I have not decided I am leaving as yet. There are matters I need to discuss alone with the countess,' the lawyer protested.

'I think not, sir,' Zed said, and stepped aside to allow Withershaws to leave the room.

'You'll regret this treatment, my lady. Remember how you fared in Wales.' The man left with as much dignity as he could garner from straightening his shirt cuffs and consulting his gold pocket watch before setting off ahead of Zed. 'Other women have been brought to book.'

His parting shot hung on the air, but Melissa could think only of his reference to Wales. She gasped, and Joanie shooed the men out of the room before bringing her a small glass of brandy from a decanter Mrs Gunn kept in the drawing room. She sipped the

fiery liquid and closed her eyes. Wales!
A lifetime away, and yet less than five
years.

★　★　★

The wind howled and sent clouds
scudding across a troubled sky. Almost
as troubled as the world below, Melissa
thought. She shrank from the casebows
in the Welsh castle when they rattled
and let rain spit through onto the
window seats. Neville had been dead
for nearly a month, and it was now
clear she did not carry his heir. His
distant cousin, Charles, would inherit
without encumbrance.

The door opened and Joanie came in
with Simmerton. She saw instantly the
defensive way they held themselves.
What now?

'Simmerton, you have a visiting card
on that tray.'

'My lady.' The butler bowed and
passed the tray across the space
between them. She lifted the embossed

card and turned it around in her fingers. 'He was most insistent with the men in the gatehouse, my lady, and eventually they allowed him up the drive into the castle.'

'I will see Mr Withershaws, Simmerton. Show him through.'

Joanie fidgeted around the room until Melissa wondered whether the girl had drunk too much ale with her breakfast. Nothing escaped her touch as she picked up and set down ornaments and cushions.

'Joanie, what ails you?'

'I beg pardon, my lady. I am disappointed, I think. I had hoped this month would be the start . . . '

'Enough,' Melissa snapped as, too late, she realised Simmerton and her guest were inside the door of the parlour. Simmerton retreated.

'Good morning, Lady Pateley,' Withershaws said. He allowed his gaze to linger hungrily on her face before he made his bow, and Melissa quelled an inward shudder. She knew that look.

Beautiful women the nation over knew it. Melissa had been subjected to it from the most unlikely personages since her husband's death. She had the fleeting impression of being a prey animal since she became a widow.

'As your uncle Walter Flaxxe's lawyer, I humbly request an hour or two of your time, ma'am. I was waiting at the inn in the village where I had retained a room. Most unsatisfactory . . . '

'Forgive my interrupting, Mr Withershaws, but I am hardly responsible for the state of any country inn you choose to patronise,' Melissa snapped, and instantly regretted the outburst. Withershaws was the sort who would harbour grudges with relish. She softened her tone a little. 'You must surely understand why I do not offer lodgings here. It's mere weeks since Neville's horrid, painful death. I feel I can only house family members at present.'

Withershaws straightened and began

to cross the floor. His booted feet clanged, and Melissa glanced down. His bowed legs reminded her somewhat of a toad.

'I more than understand, my lady. Indeed, my sister Mrs Smythe reminded me before I set off from Newcastle that young women in a delicate condition needed nurturing by their nearest and dearest relatives. While I am not a relative, I do represent your esteemed and, I'm sure, much loved uncle, Walter Flaxxe.' His voice held even less appeal than it had on the few occasions she'd met him previously in the company of her uncles. She resolved to curtail this visit as soon as possible.

'Mr Withershaws,' she said, and gestured towards the seating around the fireplace. Logs crackled in the grate, spitting sparks and flames in equal measure, but a screen protected the rugs from assault.

Withershaws waited for her to sit and then sat himself. He was not a tall man, and Melissa thought his complexion unhealthy.

'My lady, although I have written, may I repeat my sincere condolences over the death of your husband. He was shaping up into a fine man under your ladyship's guidance.'

Melissa drew a sharp breath and fixed the toad with a skewering gaze. Withershaws's opposition to Neville had been unassailable during his life, but surely common decency dictated a softening of attitude in death?

'I cannot think why you have come here, sir. If you merely wish to insult my late husband as you did during his lifetime, then you could do so by letter. Joanie, find Simmerton to see this man out.'

'One moment, your ladyship. I was opposed to the late earl, it is true, and I see no perceptible reason to change that attitude now. He would not have been your family's choice of husband . . . '

'Mr Withershaws! You outrun my patience and my tolerance. I will not discuss my marriage with you. If you have any genuine matter of business, I will hear you. Otherwise, sir, I bid you good day.'

'Ever the grande dame,' Withershaws said, and Melissa bristled. She stood up and he followed. 'However, I do have a matter of importance to discuss with your ladyship. Alone.'

'I cannot think of any reason I would consent to be alone with you, Mr Withershaws. What is your business, sir? And be quick. I expect the heir and his family during the course of this afternoon.'

'My business concerns George Gunn.'

Melissa hesitated, and in that moment Withershaws shooed Joanie out of the room. It was the clicking of the latch that brought her back into the present.

'George Gunn,' she repeated bleakly.

16

'So, my man, tell me that again, if you'd be so guid.'

Harry took a deep breath and surveyed Thomas Paxton over the rim of his tankard. He'd rarely known his friend to display such obtuseness and downright idiocy.

'Forgive me, Thomas, but what is it that ails your understanding? Melissa Pateley is lying to me. We have conducted enough interrogations when soldiering to work out when a suspect is lying and Lady Pateley is lying.'

'Calmly, man.' Thomas moved his bulk from one elbow to the other. Fortunately the table was made of thick wood and did not crack. 'I cannot think you have been obtaining information from the lady in quite the way we went about it when — '

'Thomas,' Harry growled in warning,

but his friend scarcely paused.

'My apologies, sir. Of course you heated no ironmongery, nor did you tie her wrists and ankles and drape her over the end of a — '

'Thomas Paxton, you have abandoned your wits at the bottom of that tankard,' Harry flung the accusation at his friend's head, and stood up. He paced a little, but the small back room of the tavern they'd holed up in was too confined to permit of much and he soon gave it up.

'I have my wits intact, thank ye, but I think your own are to let. The lady is unlikely to tell you her past history with that villainous, venomous apology for a man, Withershaws, without ye applying some pressure.' Thomas glanced across to the opening door and stopped talking.

They waited while the landlord had trays of food brought in. The aroma of roasted fowl swirled around them, and Harry became conscious of how very hungry he was. Two days in the saddle had carried him around the villages surrounding the city, and he'd stopped to eat here where Thomas had joined him. Tonight they planned to slide back into the old town.

'You think I might manhandle the countess?' Harry asked in frigid disdain once they were again alone.

Thomas dropped his knife and hot gravy splashed across Harry's knuckles. 'No, sir. I think you should apply a little of what my wife would recognise as *wiles*. Tempting half-truths and smiles in the right places. Calm moments of silence. What woman can withstand a moment of silence? Damn me, Harry Gunn, all the things you were so good at as a serving officer.'

'I lose the ability in her presence.'

'Ah! My wife thought that might be the case.'

Harry swallowed a large helping of chicken and quickly drank some beer to cool his mouth. He had acknowledged the weakness. It did not feel as he had thought it might, but instead he lifted sparkling hazel eyes and smiled at his companion.

'Is that how *you* knew?'

'That Agnes was more than a match for me? It is,' Thomas said, and made a wry grin. 'It is.'

'Sadly,' Harry said as reality descended in its black cloud again, 'It cannot matter, because I cannot expect to marry the lady.'

'Damn nonsense, Harry Gunn. You are allowing romantic sensibilities to obscure your judgement.' Thomas grabbed a hunk of bread and mopped around the platter he'd cleared of its meat. 'Lottie's secret was known to a few — the midwife, yer mama's maid and some of the Duart clan. All dead or implicated in the legal fraud caused by substituting one boy bairn for another.'

'When you put it in such a workmanlike manner . . . ' Harry trailed off. 'I cannot but believe it hides another axe-blow.'

'That might be the result of drinking too much of this substandard ale. We need to get back into my town-house and find ourselves some decent uisge beatha.'

'Indeed,' Harry conceded. 'However, I would be happier if Lady Pateley had told me the whole of her history with Withershaws.'

'It would be a most unhappy circumstance if he were to get hold of the details of your birth,' Thomas agreed with the words Harry wasn't saying. 'But, sir, why or how should he?'

★　★　★

Melissa, Mrs Gunn and Lottie picked their way carefully along George Square towards the junction of its northern end with Crichton Street and Charles Street. They were summoned to dine with Colonel and Mrs Paxton, accompanied by Zed and a veritable platoon. Percy and Matt carried stout wooden cudgels, and the man Leslie held the leashes of two snarling hounds.

'I am most surprised that Mrs Paxton

asks us again so soon after her party,' Mrs Gunn said. 'On the other hand, it is very pleasant to go about even if we don't have Harry to escort us.'

'It is pleasant, Mama,' Lottie agreed, but Melissa sensed an underlying hesitation. She felt sure Lottie regretted their absence had prevented them meeting Mr Withershaws face to face. 'I cannot see why we need to be escorted by all these retainers, however. They reek of the soap manufacturing.'

'We are there, my dear.' Mrs Gunn stopped at the foot of the short flight of stone steps leading up to Agnes and Thomas's front door, and accepted Zed's arm to assist her.

'Ladies, ladies,' Thomas boomed when they entered the front hall. 'Agnes is above.' They turned to the sweeping old-fashioned stair, but Thomas laid a hand on Melissa's arm.

'A moment, ma'am. Your family have sent a messenger with one or two papers to peruse. If you wouldn't mind doing this small task before dinner? A signature, I believe.'

'Of course not, Colonel Paxton. Why did he come here instead of to Mrs Gunn's house?' Melissa asked the question in all innocence, but she saw the muscles in Lottie's back bunch and relax as if she, too, thought it rather strange.

'I think he called there first, ma'am, and on being informed the ladies were going out, made an arrangement with Simmerton.'

'Indeed?'

'Yes,' the colonel said with a decided snap, and indicated a short passage to the left of the hallway. 'If you would walk along, Lady Pateley.'

Melissa did as her host bid, and a servant opened a door which let her into a room furnished as a library. It was on the east of the house, and so rather dim, but candles and lamps had been lit and a small fire burned cheerily in the grate.

'Good evening, my lady.'

'Harry!' The word escaped with the

remainder of her breath as she caught sight of who the 'messenger' was. She scanned his face to see whether the bruising was healed and was pleased to see it was no worse. What, she wondered, had brought him back?

'You changed your plans,' she accused.

Harry seemed curiously reluctant to speak again, and Melissa turned, expecting to find Thomas behind her. She would enlist his help, but Thomas was not there. They were alone.

'There are no papers in need of signing.' She moved restlessly. What had promoted such secrecy? Had there been another incident?

'I left the city, but was reluctant to stray too far when Zed had caught wind of Withershaws's arrival, and sent word,' Harry said; and she knew he watched her as carefully as the dim lighting permitted. She schooled her features, but the lawyer's name had made her start as it always did when she heard it suddenly.

'The man had the impudence to call. No doubt your spies have already informed you,' she said.

'No doubt. They would be useless spies if they did not inform.' He paced the floor, picking up a book then setting it down. 'But none of them can explain, and I find I cannot see my way further into your affairs unless I hear an explanation.'

'As to that, sir, I have made it clear there is nothing to be said about the man. My uncle is frail and will not survive more than a few months, I believe. At that time, the family will unite and wrench all our affairs back under control.'

'You are thrawn.'

'Thrawn! How can you throw such an accusation at my head?' Melissa trembled with fury. The force of his accusation touched something within her. David Withershaws was evil, but he was clever and he had made her think she could not unburden her secret to anyone; least of all to Harry Gunn, whose own life was overshadowed by the same sin.

'I say thrawn, but I mean to have the truth — and from you, my dear.'

'I will never reveal — '

'So there *is* something to reveal?'

Too late, Melissa remembered how their last conversation ended. She had claimed with some heat that Withershaws was only after control of the Flaxxe money. She had hesitated when he suggested there was more. She raised stricken eyes to his, seeing the laughter gleaming in their hazel depths. He'd tricked her, and because she was so unsure of which secrets she should keep and which she should deny without even considering whether they should be kept or shared, it was infuriating.

'My hostess must wonder where I have wandered off to. Signing papers takes only a moment.' She turned to the door, and Harry caught up with her to stretch around and open it. His smell enveloped her and teased her senses, but she would not say anything further.

His arm encircled her waist and the other slid below her knees, lifting her from the floor. Zed, ever-present Zed, waited in the corridor, and they all three left by the back stairs. Harry struggled to squeeze his bulk through the door and onto the enclosed staircase without catching her head, but she was not injured, and they were soon in the basement area at the back of the house.

'Another abduction?' she asked in withering tones that had no effect on her captor unless she counted the shaking of his shoulders, which might have been mirth.

'You said yourself, ma'am, it's open season on abducting the countess. I do not like to be backward in any attentions a lady expects.' They had reached the lane, and Harry set off towards George Square. 'I will carry you till we reach cleaner flags. Evening shoes are not at all suitable for this unswept area.'

'In truth, my dear, I simply want a little time to persuade you of the importance of telling me what it is that turns Withershaws's name into the Sword of Damocles.'

Melissa stilled then. Oh yes, that was exactly what Withershaws's had become. They were now standing in the hall of Harry's house. They'd come in through the basement, where the corridor doors were all unusually closed, but Zed was ahead of them on the stairs with a candle.

'In here, my lady,' Zed said as he opened the door of the dining room. The shutters had been closed, and Harry lit a few candles while Zed set his down and lit a lamp. He left, and Melissa heard the door close onto its latch.

'The door in the castle closed onto a latch,' she said, and watched as if in a dwam while Harry slowly straightened and turned to gaze on her. She sank onto a small sofa, grateful for the solid bulk below her knees.

Harry chose a carver chair and sat down quietly. Melissa looked at his beautiful features still marred by bruising, but shadowed and mysterious in the lamplight. What did it matter any longer? she wondered. Had the keeping of secrets not marred more lives than they would have destroyed?

'Withershaws came calling in Wales. He came exactly four weeks after Neville's death and tricked Joanie into leaving him alone with me in the Great Chamber. It was the door clicking onto the latch that alerted me then.' She glanced again at Harry's dear face, and could not make out whether he thought she and Joanie had been fools or genuinely tricked by an evil and unscrupulous male.

She drew a shaky breath and felt sweat gathering along her upper lip. This was such a difficult story to tell, and Harry was so silent. So silent and patient.

'He shot the bolt. He crossed the room with slow steps, most deliberate, and stopped close to me. Too close for a real gentleman who had concern for the comfort of a lady.'

Involuntarily, Melissa lifted her left hand and fiddled with the curls of her wig. She tugged and the thing shifted a little. She eased it back onto her crown. Joanie would despair.

'I realised, perhaps had realised as soon as the man entered the chamber, what he had in mind, but I was still very shocked by Neville's sudden death. He reached out and gripped the neck of my gown with both his ink-stained hands. He would have ripped it apart, but I was holding a water glass, and I broke it on the table he'd trapped me against and forced it between us.'

It had all happened at great speed; and even now, Melissa was hard pressed to say how her instincts had snapped into life. But they had, and the man was stayed for a moment or two.

'He said I wouldn't injure him,

wouldn't use such a weapon on him, my uncle's esteemed lawyer. I hesitated of course, and he grabbed my wrist. Although he was puny in comparison with the young men in Neville's circle, he was strong enough to force me to drop the glass, and he grinned in triumph.' She sat back against the padded rest of the sofa. 'He was quite, quite mad. His eyes bulged with — '

'Lust,' Harry said.

'Rapine, Colonel. He told me then that he'd heard Joanie say I was not with child, and he intended to rectify that.'

'I don't understand, Melissa,' Harry said calmly, ignoring her formal 'Colonel'. 'Do you mean he would impregnate you and make the world believe the bairn was Neville's?'

'Yes.' The stark word held agony. 'Yes. He thought to make me pregnant and thus have me, and the title, under his control.'

'The title,' Harry mused aloud. 'What if the bairn was a girl?'

'The man was mad in his pursuit of power, Harry. None of these rational thoughts would have held any interest for him.'

'Did he . . . did you . . . '

Melissa quailed at the sound of Harry's uncertainty. How could she blame him? 'He did not succeed. Joanie led one of the castle's guards into the chamber through a door from the kitchens, and he was ejected before he could even rip my dress off.'

'It is very clear why his name makes you pale, my dear. But, Melissa, none of this was your fault in any way. Why have you not told your uncle of it?'

'Withershaws got to my uncle first. He made a plausible tale of a lovelorn woman in need of male comfort who had thrown herself at him, and with the help of a shard of glass had tried to have him assist her in creating an heir where none existed.' She lifted her head from contemplation of the embroidery down the front of her gown. Harry's expression was one of total mystification.

'My dear, no one who had met your late husband would think of you throwing yourself onto Withershaws.' He straightened those long muscular legs, and it brought a small smile to her lips. 'But we must recognise that not everyone sees themselves as others see them,' he added. 'It's a sentiment addressed by Rabbie Burns, I think.'

'Harry, it needs to be remembered that I threw myself onto Neville against my family's advice, and also . . . ' She paused. Was it an indelicate remark she needed to make? 'Also, my uncle is elderly, but he likes to remember his younger days when he considered himself as something of a ladies' man. He may not see Withershaws as an undesirable person where they are concerned.'

'He saw him as an attractive prospect to a widow.'

'Withershaws always believed I married Neville to become a countess, whereas I married Neville because I could not contemplate life without him. I would have married Neville if he had been a coal hewer.'

'Well, I cannot think how you would have met him had he been a coal hewer, but I take your point. You think that because Withershaws wants to be in and of the ton, he cannot see how anyone might not want that goal?'

'It is true. He is consumed by the desire to lift himself out of his class into the ton.' She sat quietly then, mulling over the last few moments. It was good to have shared this harrowing tale with someone other than Joanie. She felt easier somehow; more relaxed. *Perhaps*, she thought, *it is because he does not condemn me as my uncle did so promptly.*

'So Withershaws wished to gain control of the earldom by first creating the earl and then marrying his mother.' Harry's cool tones interrupted Melissa's reflections. 'Where into all of this does my cousin George fit?'

'George was already making a minor

nuisance. He had to be escorted from the funeral service when he insinuated himself into the family pews. It was unseemly.'

'Where did you first encounter him?'

'First?' Melissa was puzzled. 'In truth, I cannot tell, Harry. He was sufficient nuisance that when Withershaws brought up his name in Wales, I was distracted, and he was able to get Joanie out of the room.'

'I begin to wonder whether George's interest in you has ever been independent of Withershaws's malign manipulation.'

'Another way of gaining control of the title?' Melissa pondered. 'But the title is now beyond keeping. I am the Countess of Pateley, as Charles has no wife, and I will become the Dowager after Charles's son inherits and his wife takes it. Should I marry, I would not pass it on to my husband or my children.' She hesitated. 'In some respects, I'm more than ready to become a plain Mrs — ' 'Mrs Gunn' was what she wanted to say, but not what Harry wanted to hear.

'Willingly, my dear?'

'I did not marry Neville for his title.'

'That is not the question I am asking.' Harry's expressive eyes darkened as he waited for her answer. 'Will you willingly become Mrs Gunn when I might become a penniless and landless bastard at any moment?'

It tore the breath from Melissa to hear his circumstances described so starkly, but she held his gaze and replied as steadily as she could.

'Why, sir, I have had offers for my hand made in more attractive terms.' She smiled a little and nodded. 'I would consider myself the most fortunate of women to become Mrs Gunn.'

In an instant, Harry had crossed the space between them and snatched her up. His bulk wrapped her round, and Melissa felt him tremble. She was clasped so tightly that she could not reach back to look into his face, and was struggling to breathe before he relaxed his hold and dropped a deep kiss on her upturned lips.

'You make me the happiest of men, my dear.'

17

'I think there should not be an announcement of our betrothal at present, Mama,' Harry said. They were gathered in the drawing room late the following morning. Mrs Gunn, Lottie, Kitty, Mairie, Agnes and Thomas Paxton occupied chairs and sofas, while Melissa sat in the window and Harry paced.

'Of course, my dear. I would wish you to inform your aunt and relatives in Newcastle, in case they fear there is anything less than honourable about it.'

Melissa had watched her newly betrothed quarter the carpet and measure its length and breadth with all the purpose of a regimental sergeant. It was at best unnerving.

'Harry, please sit down,' Lottie protested. 'You are making me dizzy as I try to hear your arguments, and poor

Mama cannot always catch words that are thrown over one's shoulder.'

Melissa sent Lottie a grateful smile, but the other woman turned away. There had been a lot of hilarity and many congratulations the previous evening when the ladies returned from dining at the Paxtons' house. Only Lottie had seemed a little subdued, and this morning the coldness of her demeanour was unmistakeable. Melissa wondered whether she did not approve.

'I think Lottie has a point, Harry,' Melissa said mildly. 'I also think my relatives will welcome you into the family. They are already grateful that your dealings through the Edinburgh lawyers have resulted in changes for their pensioners.'

'That's one issue among many.' Harry's reply was terse and he sat down heavily, causing his mama to raise an eyebrow when the chair slid backwards a couple of inches.

'Harry, there will be grooves in the parquet,' Mrs Gunn remonstrated.

Melissa saw Harry stiffen and sent an enquiring glance to Thomas Paxton. Did he, as she now did, think there was more to be learned from Lottie's impenetrable silence than would come out in front of the younger women? She watched the muscles flex across his face as this older man, Harry's mentor in so many ways, gathered his thoughts and made an imperceptible nod.

'Agnes, did you not mention to me that you wished Kitty and Mairie might see the new schoolroom you have established in Charles Street?' Colonel Paxton said lazily. He stirred in his chair, and after a moment or two of shuffling succeeded in lifting himself onto his feet. His wife was forced to rise also in the face of her husband's clear signal. Melissa watched the war of emotions chasing across her pretty face.

'I did, Paxton, but they may wish to remain here while such new family business is being discussed,' Agnes said, striving to delay their departure. But the younger ladies were both very interested in the new schoolroom and possibly, Melissa thought, influenced by the stern expression on Harry's face.

'Why Mrs Paxton, you are always able to have the tradesmen move more quickly than any of us. I am hopeful that the new baby will be a girl, and I would so love to see how you have organised the rooms,' Kitty said. She rose, and twirling her parasol, walked a little towards the door. Mairie followed, and within a very few moments Melissa was alone with Harry, Mrs Gunn and Lottie. A charged silence settled over them.

★　★　★

'I cannot pretend, Mama, that I am in favour of this match, and so I will say without dissembling that I am not.'

The chill words dripped into the room, and Melissa lifted her head. She remembered how Harry had prophesied this woman might still cause trouble for them, and it appeared to be coming true.

'You have carried out a far greater pretence over many years, Lottie,' Harry answered. 'Why should a little thing like who I marry make your powers fail?'

'That is a monstrous remark,' Mrs Gunn interrupted. 'I had thought you were nurtured to show more forgiveness to others weaker than yourself, sir.'

Melissa saw how the words made Harry's complexion fire, but he did not apologise or retract them. She turned her head and caught a look of such despair in Lottie's face that she was startled into standing up.

'Lottie what is it that makes you so despairing?'

'No doubt she's realised how the present arrangements deprive her *respectable* son of the lairdship,' Harry said, ignoring his mother's plea for forbearance.

'I don't think they do, Harry. Duart said his papa was very careful over the drafting of my father's will and the dispositions it contained. You are in an unassailable position as the owner of all the lands and property. A scandal would send nothing Alexander's way, not even the title.' Melissa realised how carefully her future sister had thought through the implications.

'Then what can your objections be?' Harry asked in exasperation.

'My objections are that we do not know for certain who your papa was.'

Melissa sat down again and took a deep breath. What did Lottie mean? Had there been more than one unspeakable rogue? Involuntarily, her hand rose to cover her mouth.

'Lottie,' Mrs Gunn said feebly, 'what can you mean?'

'I mean the man who stole my honour may have given us a false name.' Lottie kept her clear hazel gaze fixed on Harry, but he was so obviously confused that Melissa might have laughed if the scene had been playing out on a stage.

'How long have you known there was a possibility of confusion?' Mrs Gunn asked. 'Roland Farquar was the name you told me.'

'Papa searched carefully for the villain, but he never established that any person of that name existed. In time he gave up, and as the man was never seen again, his identity slipped from our minds and concerns,' Lottie said.

'Then why now?' Melissa asked, despite every fibre of her being resisting the answer she knew was coming. Somehow, George and Withershaws were involved.

'I have had a letter from the man, David Withershaws.'

'Mr Withershaws wrote to you?' Melissa was scandalised by his daring. 'He showed unforgiveable presumption.'

'And how did he know?' Harry asked.

'I do not know how he found out, Harry, because it has been a very well-guarded secret.' Lottie paled even more, and Melissa watched as a tear slid down each of her cheeks. Lottie shook her head, though, and continued. 'He suggests that my Roland Farquar was Richard Flaxxe. Your papa in fact, Lady Pateley,' Lottie concluded bleakly.

'No.' Harry shouted the word. Melissa heard it resonate off the walls as she slid to the floor.

★   ★   ★

Harry cradled Melissa in his arms as she came round from her fainting fit. The warm body was relaxed in unconsciousness, and he could not rid himself of the memory of that night when he had held her in her sleep until the nightmares receded. Was that to be the only time he shared a bed with her?

'She's opening her eyes, Harry,' Lottie spoke quietly, and he appreciated her assistance in lifting the countess onto a sofa. Mama brought over a glass of water and waited till he was able to take it from her and hold it to Melissa's lips.

It was going to be the devil's own work sorting out this mess, Harry thought. No wonder Lottie had been so opposed to the betrothal and so keen for George to be successful.

'Take your time, Melissa,' he said as she struggled to sit unaided and shrugged out of his arms. Did she already find him untouchable?

'Mrs Duart, I am appalled. Can you not see this is yet another of Withershaws's ploys?' So, not him, but Lottie was to feel the brunt of her anger. Harry found it was not as consoling as he wished.

'Melissa, we cannot condemn Lottie for this. Rather she would have been doing a great wrong to keep the information to herself,' he said and hoped it sounded more neutral than he felt.

'But she must know who the man she lay with was. How is it possible she does not?' Melissa asked with passion.

'Of course it's possible. The handsome stranger chooses the same initials as his own name, and so his belongings are all marked with RF. He does not seek society because he wants to . . .' Harry took a deep breath and forced himself to continue. He took no pleasure in outlining how his sister-mama must have been seduced, but they had to be straight now. 'Because he wants to seduce the young lady and move on. Lottie, I am sorry to be so blunt, but we must be as honest as possible.'

'You are very calm, sir. Perhaps you already regret your offer of marriage,' Melissa said in tones of cold fury. Harry was little surprised, but it did not make matters any simpler or easier.

'My dear, you are shocked, and it will be some while before your sensibilities recover. There is nothing I regret in our relations. We must hope to resolve Withershaws's allegations, but shouting at each other is exactly what the man wants to achieve.'

'Of course he does,' Melissa said, and the fight left her as suddenly as it had arrived. 'Of course.'

Harry smoothed tiny curls now covering Melissa's scalp. Her wig had come off when she fell and none of them thought to retrieve it.

'There may be ways to establish whether your papa travelled in Scotland at the time I was got . . . '

'I knew as soon as Melissa's name was brought to mind,' Mrs Gunn said, and Harry suppressed a groan.

'Mama, you remembered how very flaxen my hair was and that it emphasised how different I looked from George,' he said. He had wondered about his mother's fainting fit, but disregarded it when she explained how Lottie was his real mama. He hadn't then looked any deeper. Clearly, he would have to be more military-minded if he was to sort out this mess. Disregarding evidence was not the best policy.

'After so many years, Harry, how do

you propose to proceed?' Lottie said.

'I will brief Zed and we will consult with Thomas. That's usually a good place to begin.'

'But perhaps not in his house,' Melissa said. 'That is how Agnes found out, and it may be how Withershaws learned of it, too.'

'I think not, Lady Pateley,' Lottie said quietly. 'While I agree that the walls of Thomas Paxton's house conceal nothing when the gentlemen become excited. The lawyer wrote to me before I set off for Lauder in response to Harry's request for help.'

'This is why you were receptive to George's approach?' Melissa asked.

'Yes.'

Harry recognised the bleakness of his sister's response and did not pursue any of the arguments and questions raging through his brain. He thought they might never learn how Withershaws got hold of the details. Although he and Thomas had discounted any of the principals in the affair disclosing it, there must have been others. Was the minister's wife suspicious and scandalised? In a house where so many babies were born and where a son was so wanted, how could the general servants not have realised Lottie's condition? Who had the midwife been, and who were her relatives? The possibilities were many.

'A man like this must be always on the lookout for scandal and gossip. He will have antennae waving in every breeze to catch what he can and what he thinks might be useful to him,' he said at last. None of his ladies responded.

18

Melissa kept to her room during the rest of that day, but by dinner-time she was heartily sick of her own company.

'Joanie, I will go down to eat with the household. Was my amber gown among the items the men threw into our boxes?'

'Yes, my lady. It's hanging just inside the cupboard,' Joanie replied, and Melissa thought she detected a trace of relief in the girl's voice. Harry and Zed had been absent from the house all day, and Lottie had departed for her own townhouse across in Queen Street. Possibly Mrs Duart, her mama-in-law, would appreciate her company while they waited for Duart's return from his abandoned sea-trip. And possibly not, Melissa reflected sadly.

'I suppose Mrs Duart thinks she'll be less likely to tell any of the secret if she is out of her sisters' hearing,' Melissa mused and heard Joanie's sharp intake of breath. 'I cannot dissemble any longer, Joanie. I know you will have worked out what this latest setback is founded on. I suppose, too, that Zed will have explained much of our trouble to you.'

'He is most discreet, my lady. He said only that not all foundlings ended up in an institution,' Joanie replied, but then may have realised how very revealing a remark it was and stopped speaking on a short cough.

'Yes. He and his master may have more in common than even they realised,' Melissa said. She helped Joanie's tasks in dressing her by sitting on a low stool. The girl moved around as carefully as always. When she lifted the wig, brushed and tidied, Melissa stayed her hand.

'I have a mind to go down without it tonight.' Even as she spoke, her chest tightened and she trembled a little. It was going to take a lot of courage, but she felt the moment had arrived.

'If you say so, my lady,' Joanie replied, and set the hated thing back on a stand Mrs Gunn had found for them from a supply in the attics. 'I think they must be hot and scratchy to wear for a long time.'

'They are,' Melissa conceded as she ran her fingers over her burgeoning curls. Who did she resemble herself? she wondered. Possibly her looks came from her mama's family, as she could find no resemblance to Harry Gunn when she dared to look in the mirror.

That is no way to think. Harry Gunn is not your brother. Papa would never have done such a thing as seduce a schoolgirl. Never.

'Joanie, do you see a very close resemblance between Colonel Gunn and George Gunn?'

'Not really. They have the same jaw-line, but the mouths are different. Somehow you can tell that George Gunn will be pettish. He seems always to be waiting for you to cross him, and he purses his lips.' Joanie splashed eau de cologne around her, and Melissa breathed in the delicate bergamot scent. 'The colonel, now, he's a real man. Nothing about him that doesn't tell you he's in charge and you'd do well to listen.'

'And obey?'

'Indeed, my lady. Has the colonel been ordering you about?' Joanie seemed more animated by that thought than anything else they'd talked about during this very long day.

'Not yet. Well, not very much. But I sense there will be orders coming out of his discussion with Colonel Paxton and Zed.'

'Me, too, my lady.' Joanie stood back to survey her handiwork. Melissa watched with fascination as the girl smiled quietly and then let a huge grin cover her face. 'You know that Zed person is always saying as how we need to think ahead.'

'Yes, he does,' Melissa agreed. She wondered what her maid was leading this conversation around to.

'Well, my lady, we've been messed with a lot by these menfolk. And the ones what came courting you, courting the countess, I heard one of them say, when you were so very ill and injured.' Joanie stopped abruptly again. A tiny blush flitted across her cheeks and she took a deep breath before continuing. 'It seems to me, my lady, we ought to do something.'

'Something, Joanie?' Melissa asked faintly. 'I'm not fit enough to go cantering around the countryside asking old retainers whether they think the laird resembles . . . ' Melissa stopped. Her brain churned with the force of the thoughts pulsing in it. 'But other people are fit, and other people are very likely to be visiting Berwick Old Abbey on the way to Edinburgh.'

'My lady?'

Before Melissa could share her idea with the maid, there was a sharp knock on the door. Through the panelling she heard Harry's voice.

'Lady Pately, I hope you will allow me to escort you down to dinner.'

Mistress and maid exchanged amused glances. Ordering was what Harry was good at, but they had their own ideas.

★   ★   ★

'Agnes, may I ask a favour of you?' Melissa sat with Agnes on a wooden settle in front of the huge windows that faced the square. They were drinking tea and watching the men huddle together over a map spread across the sofa table. Mrs Gunn had retired, pleading a headache and her advanced age, so the two younger women were on their own.

'A favour? That sounds enticing. I do hope it's comprised of a little danger and the chance to stab Mr David Withershaws. I speak metaphorically of course,' Agnes added.

'Metaphorically? Someone is very

likely to end that villain's life prematurely, but let us hope it will not be one of our circle.' Melissa set her cup onto its saucer and collected her thoughts. They had been sorely tried throughout the meal as the men lunged and parried over the best way to defeat Withershaws and his acolyte, George Gunn.

'As you say, Melissa, our society is small enough that we do not want any to be transported or hanged.' She shuddered and Melissa did, too. Withershaws was just the sort of individual whose unreasonable behaviour drove sane men to despairing action.

'Let us hope our menfolk can be prevented from taking any precipitate action. It is why I need a favour,' Melissa said as calmly as she could, but the excitement of her ideas was almost too difficult to resist. 'Can you spare a man to ride to my home outside Berwick?'

'The Old Abbey? Why, yes, I could arrange with Thomas . . . '

'No,' Melissa interrupted forcibly,

and startled Agnes. 'I beg your pardon, Agnes, but I feel this is an arrangement Thomas and Harry, and very particularly, Zed, should know nothing of.'

'I see. No, I don't in fact. Why are we acting like thieves in the night?' A tiny frown of puzzlement furrowed her brow, and she twitched her nose as if sniffing out a bad smell. Melissa tried not to laugh.

'I do not believe the men would accede to my plan, and it's so very simple that it deserves the chance to succeed.' Melissa smiled wryly at her friend.

'Certainly, the men do not enjoy simple. Simple seems to be an affront to their military backgrounds,' Agnes agreed thoughtfully. She straightened and, glancing across at her lord, smiled. 'Thomas would be most surprised to learn of the machinations I go through in order to help him feel he has solved problems for me.'

'Neville had those sort of tendencies in his nature, although we were married for such a short time, they hardly had much opportunity to blossom,' Melissa said. She composed her thoughts at last and explained them to Agnes. 'My idea is this. My mama was a little vain, and during the twenty years of her marriage, she had a portrait painted every year. Sometimes she was alone, but on several occasions she was with my papa. There is a half-size painting of my parents drawn in 1793 which I consider to be a good likeness of them both.'

'And you think to have it brought to Edinburgh?' Agnes was excited, too.

'I do. I think if Lottie could see it, she would be able to say once and for all that my papa was not the villain who seduced her.' Melissa spoke with all the warmth her papa's memory always stirred in her. 'I knew him for sixteen years, Agnes. I know he could not have done such a terrible thing.'

Her friend reached across and patted her hands gently. 'Of course you do. It is too easy to be distracted by the shouting of others. We must remember what we knew the person to be like.'

'Thank you, Agnes.'

'Now, my young cousin, Murdo Mainland will be lounging about, as he has recently decided not to return to his studies in the university. I will visit his mama's, where he is likely to be found at present, and make an arrangement,' Agnes said, and it was very business-like. 'You will furnish me with the details of where this portrait may be found. I imagine the Old Abbey is a large building?'

★   ★   ★

The ladies might have been less sanguine in their planning had they caught sight of Harry Gunn's interested glances straying their way from time to time. He had been occupied all day with Thomas and Zed and then their family lawyers to the extent that his brain began to feel full. He now struggled to follow Zed's finger as it traced across the map of Lothianshire.

Indeed, Harry wondered, what did it serve them to know where Withershaws was? His physical being was nothing like as dangerous as his knowledge.

'Enough,' he said at last, and the others looked up. Zed's expression was quizzical, but Thomas looked relieved, Harry thought. It had been a long day for both of them, too.

'I agree, Harry,' Thomas said. 'We are gaining nothing except headache by poring over these things. Zed, have there been any more reports from our men?'

'Not since you dined, sir. Leslie will be out among the crowds coming from the ale-houses later on, and Donal has an assignation with a woman known to be favoured by the visitor from the south,' Zed said without any expression. 'She's known as Highland Nell.'

Harry smiled wryly. It would be some kind of poetic justice if they were to track the man to a brothel, he supposed. He had not thought Withershaws would seek out such company, but Melissa's sorry tale of his behaviour in Wales suggested he had red-blooded fervour when roused. Would besting them over the knowledge of Harry's parenting drive him out to seek female company?

'Perhaps we should escort Agnes home and then make our own way to Rose Street,' Thomas said with more than a twinkle in his eye. Shards of light flashed as they had done so often before an engagement in the wars. Harry knew he was spoiling for a fight, but hoped the strenuous walk through the town might calm him down. He could not contemplate an expedition through those thronged streets by himself. It was one thing to send Donal in working clothes, although even that could prove chancy.

'Thomas, we are likely to be recognised,' he said. 'The men know how to don rags and rub in some of the ingredients from the soap-making so they are both filthy and noxious. No one will look twice at Donal even with his empty sleeve.'

'And what will it profit us to find Withershaws tonight, sir?' Zed asked carefully. They knew of old how Thomas could be driven toward something of interest when you were actually trying to steer him away. 'Surely Donal's mission is to follow the villain and find out where he lodges?'

'That may well be Donal's mission, but we are not so nice that an encounter in a dark pend would not be welcome,' Thomas shot back. Harry rolled up the map and gestured to Percy, who was on duty.

'Return this to my study.' He waited while the young man left the room and glanced again at the ladies where they sat, still immersed in conversation. Uneasy prickles crawled all over Harry's scalp. Not only was Thomas a little too far in his liquor, but the women were clearly plotting something that pleased them very well. He remembered Melissa's excursion to the Lawnmarket which ended badly enough, and thought he would lock all the house's doors from the outside if he left it tonight.

'Thomas, it is no intention of mine to assault anyone, even a villain like Withershaws. It will not serve our ends in this matter if we have to spend hours arguing our case in front of their worthy lordships,' he protested. 'I do sympathise. There's nothing I'd enjoy more than landing one in that bully's smug face.'

'Besides, neither of you have set eyes on the man yet,' Zed said with the calmness of logic. 'You might very well land one on the wrong lawyer.'

'Is it only lawyers who frequent the brothels, then, Zed?' Harry heard Thomas's question with growing impatience. It, too, had logic, but it was the sort of logic displayed by the drunk. He suppressed a groan. How had he failed to watch Thomas's consumption as the evening wore on? Why had he carelessly suggested a sortie?

'I think not, Colonel. I think not. But

my point is valid whether you land one on a wrong lawyer or a wrong minister of the kirk. It won't do.'

'I don't know why you retain this man, Harry. He's capable of spoiling any night's good sport.' Thomas belched then and Harry saw Agnes's head lift and the flush of irritation suffuse her features. Perhaps a man should not wait too long before giving up his bachelor status and taking the civilising influence of a wife. It was a sobering thought, and one that stirred the impatience he was fighting. He needed to know whether Melissa was his half-sister so he could bring this intolerable stage of his life to an end.

'Thomas, Zed and I will escort you and your beautiful wife home, and then I think we'll need to visit the stables.'

'The stables?' Thomas asked. Harry could see his fuddled senses trying to grasp the huge leap from villainous lawyers to stables.

'Why, yes. Zed reported that Gorse was showing lame earlier today. I will not sleep comfortably without I see how the groom is treating him. He's altogether more important than a horny little pest from Newcastle. Wouldn't you say?' Harry hoped his friend was far gone enough to let things go without more exertion.

'Indeed. Gorse is a fine chap. I hope you find him well, Harry. Would you like my advice on any matter?'

'I think not, Thomas. Of course if he has made no progress tomorrow, then I will ask for your advice.'

19

Melissa watched the men collect their heavy overcoats from Simmerton in the front hallway. She was a few steps up from the floor and out of the bustle. She watched how they lifted walking sticks from the huge tub kept in readiness and tested each by raising it and lowering it until they settled on one with a weight that matched their strength. It was a worrying sight because it told her more clearly than any words that they expected to need protection as they walked.

Percy was bundled into a half-coat of dark-coloured bombazine and Matt kitted out with rags. She did hope Harry knew what he was about. Matt, to her mind, considered himself to be a rather elegant person and wouldn't relish looking like someone scratching out an existence among the flea-ridden shapes that stirred in the shadows of Edinburgh's streets.

'Give me the house keys, Simmerton,' Harry said while taking them from the hand of the startled butler. 'Don't wait up tonight. I have secured all the entrances and barred the shutters on the windows.'

Melissa felt the breath leave her body with a mighty whoosh and she staggered against the bannister. Harry was at her side in an instant.

'My dear, what is it?'

'You're locking us in. I have already suffered one fire, surely . . . '

'Of course. How thoughtless of me. I will leave the keys for the area doors with Simmerton,' he said quietly. His warm fingers squeezed her elbow, and she let his strength flow along her nerve endings like the salves he'd used to ease her pain.

'Harry, I will not be using your absence to make any further sorties into the town,' she said. 'I know you were watching Agnes and me as we enjoyed

356

our gossiping after dinner, but we were not making such plans as you seem to think.' Melissa watched the red flare across Harry's skin and knew she'd touched the heart of his concerns. Had she said enough to placate him and divert him?

'I don't pretend to know what canker is in your brain, Gunn, but I swear I will not be wandering out of my house either,' Agnes added from the doorway where she waited with diminishing patience for the men to rig themselves out and be ready. 'Paxton, I wish to return home.'

'My dear,' the colonel murmured before making a sweeping bow to Melissa. Percy sprang forward and judiciously caught the colonel before his weight tipped him onto the granite flags.

'Thank ye, lad. Did ye ever want employment, ye must but apply to ma steward . . . '

'Paxton!' Agnes's patience snapped and Melissa let a huge grin split her face. 'I leave now, and if you wish to share my chamber tonight, you would be well advised to fall in.'

'My dear. Indelicate. Tut, tut,' the colonel muttered, but he did indeed fall in and then out the door into the dark of an autumn night.

* * *

Harry watched Zed skilfully manoeuvre Thomas Paxton up the front steps of his mansion and out of sight into the cavernous hallway. He let his gaze wander over the roof-line and saw again how one or two of the chimney heads were not quite straight. These old buildings had served well, but he felt their time was nearly up.

'He's all the way upstairs, sir,' Zed spoke at Harry's elbow. 'Mistress Paxton has agreed to lock the bedroom door when he drops asleep.'

'I cannot think that will take very long,' Harry replied. He knew where his own few men were around him in the streets and was beginning to sense where Percy was and Matt in relation to them. Although neither of Melissa's footmen had been in the military, they were shaping up well in this battle against Withershaws.

'Rose Street is it, sir?' Zed asked. 'Or what about West Nicholson Street?'

'Do you know of an attraction there?' Harry stilled his long stride, which had already been carrying him towards the north of the city and the narrow confines of Rose Street. 'My own feeling is the man will be attracted by the new buildings across the Nor' loch.'

'You may well be correct, sir, and Donal is down there somewhere. We should try to make contact with him.' Zed sounded relieved to be overruled, and Harry hoped he was right to do so. On the other hand, what was their purpose in finding the lawyer? Was it not also time to let go his soldiering instincts as Lottie kept suggesting?

Time and not yet time, he thought as they quickly dodged and jouked their way through the folk still abroad. He'd been brought up short by Zed's remark that he did not know his enemy's face. It was certainly time to put that right. He needed to see this man who was setting all their lives into such miserable disarray.

'Are you minded to take the right or left from the main thoroughfare?' Zed asked, dragging Harry back into the dark reality of their present circumstances. He drew in a lungful of noisome air laden with the smoke of late cooking fires and escaping candle grease. Right, or left? He nodded to the right and saw Zed raise a hand in that direction. It was an order their men knew. One or two would follow them into the right-hand lane and two or three would hive off to the other side meantime.

'Who has charge of Lady Pateley's men?'

'Leslie.' The word was staccato, and Harry was forced to recognise Zed's agitation. Would his loyal man rather be back in George Square? he wondered. Perhaps it was time for all of them to forego this type of night-time sortie. 'I have seen Withershaws when he intruded on the countess, but it will do no harm if he catches sight of so many weel kent faces, and he does ken Percy and Matt.'

'I agree. Let him see a little of our strength. How I wish Thomas did not drink so deeply.'

'Sir, he a'ways has. He'll be angry with hi'sel' in the dawn light.' Zed hesitated, and Harry slid further into the shadows. He hefted his stick, testing its weight again and knocking it briefly against a wall. What had the man seen? They slowed until progress was no more than a creep along the drainage ditches. Scuttling creatures fled from their boots, and one or two crows lifted into the air in a flurry of wings too dark to see but loud enough to hear.

Along the roadway, a door stood open to the night. Uncertain light spilled out, and once close enough to find an angle, they could peer into a cramped passageway with stairs leading both down and up at the far end. Two men lounged there like the guard-dogs they undoubtedly were. Within seconds, a large man in the clothing of a country gentleman picked his way onto the flags. He dipped his fingers into the pocket of his embroidered waistcoat and produced two coins which he flicked towards the guards.

Zed grunted as quietly as anyone might grunt, and Harry took that to confirm this was not their man. They kept moving, but as they reached the open door one of the guards stepped in front of Harry.

'Gae nae further, sir,' he bellowed along the road. 'We hae the tastiest morsel aboon. She'll afford anything a gent like yoursel' micht wish for.'

Harry stepped away from the wall he'd been hugging and into the roadway. He did not wish to find himself trapped with no room to swing the walking stick if he could not defuse this encounter. He lifted the stick into the guttering light of a flare above the entryway and watched the man step back.

'Noo, then guid sirs, gents of the first rank like yersel's — ' He nodded towards Zed's upright frame. ' — will be michty carefu' o' yer persons an' this lady aboon is o' the same walk in life.'

He leaned forward as if to create an intimacy between them, and Harry held himself in place, although the stench of the man's breath was almost strong enough to knock him over on its own.

'That gentleman ye wid catch sicht o' as he sauntered oot richt happy an' satisfied, is the son o' a duke. Ye'll no expect me tae say which wan, but . . . '

'We recognise Lord Youngman easily enough,' Zed hissed. 'There's a coin for ye, if ye point us towards the girl whae does weel oot o' lawyers. English lawyers. Highland Nell.'

'Whit dae gents like yersel's want wi' her? A slut an' naw mistake . . . '

363

The man's words were cut off by Zed's strong fingers grasping his neck cloth and twisting until his face turned purple and his heels began to lift from the cobbles. Harry saw the other guard begin to start forward. Out of the corner of his eye, he made out Percy's tall shape and a moving bundle of rags that might be Matt. All the same, Zed was a little precipitate, he thought.

'Let him talk, man,' Harry said. He watched the man's colour fade to bright red as Zed's hand slackened but didn't release.

'Twa doors doon on the nor,' the wretch mumbled. 'She's in demand the nicht.' He hauled himself out of Zed's grasp with a heave of his shoulders and moved back into his hallway. Just as he would think he'd reached safety, Percy's foot shot out and he fell backwards onto the floor. Zed loomed over him.

'Whae else wiz askin' aboot the girl?' Zed kept his voice low, but the local accent sent fingers of fear shivering along Harry's own nerve-ends and he saw how the second guard moved silently onto the stair at the end of the hallway.

'The first wiz a middling gentleman with an English air and a voice that wisnae local,' their informant said more willingly than when on his feet. He kept a close watch on Zed's stick, now retrieved from its belt around his waist and jiggling up and down. Zed whacked it against the entryway and slivers of plaster fell over their prisoner.

'Thank you,' Harry said. 'You will now forget you met anyone looking for him.'

'And the ithers?' Zed asked implacably.

'Wan, he wiz mair like yer man here. Gie like him, but dark an' he had the English accent tae.'

They left the entryway then and walked briskly along and beyond the door that had been pointed out to them. Percy moved even further on, Leslie slouched against the opposite wall, and Matt huddled into an alcove carved below a ground floor window. Zed relaxed as Harry watched him slot his walking stick back through the belt around his waist.

'You were worried that George would not be here?' he asked his lieutenant as the realisation crept into his brain. 'Why?'

'Sorry, sir. He makes me nervous when I don't exactly know his where-abouts or intentions. Now it's just his intentions we're unsighted over,' Zed conceded with a little reluctance.

'Yes, now we know there are likely to be two of them in her boudoir.' Harry gazed up through the gloom to a first-floor window. As he watched, the small patch of light grew and a shutter clattered against an inside wall. A woman's pale face appeared in the gap, and an unearthly shriek broke above their heads.

★   ★   ★

Melissa rose almost as soon as Joanie closed the door of her room. She slid carefully off the bed and crossed to the windows that looked out over the basement areas and the lane. The private gardens were accessed through wooden gates off the lane, and she could make out tall shapes like trees and shrubs, but nothing below that closer to ground level. There was little natural light and almost no torches or flares.

She lit a candle and sat down with a book on her lap. The words were scarcely discernible, but it soothed her agitation to have a story lying there and to stroke her fingers across the page. How strange a story her life was fashioning, she thought. Outside a dog yelped, and she lifted her head waiting for something more, but nothing came. This was intolerable. How long would she have to spend wondering whether George Gunn was lurking in her surroundings? Would it continue after she married Harry? If she married Harry?

Promises were so difficult to keep to

when circumstances changed. She had promised Harry she would not leave the house, and where would she go if she did? Certainly not down into the town where she felt certain the men had gone. Harry's talk of Gorse showing lame might have fooled a drunken Thomas Paxton, but no one else believed it.

Would it be so very bad to ease out of the house and cross the lane into the garden? She could ask Joanie to accompany her and maybe even Simmerton. Inactivity was suffocating her. Harry should understand that. He was such a vigorous individual. She rose, letting the book clatter onto the floor.

Lifting a warm shawl from the foot of the bed, she threw it around her shoulders and gripped it tightly across her front. She shucked her feet into some low-backed leather slippers and picked up the candle. Immediately, she realised it wasn't going to be possible to get downstairs in this manner. She set the candle down again and crossed to the door of her bedroom.

'Lady Pateley. Are you unwell, ma'am?' Simmerton asked as soon as she opened the door. Joanie was sitting further down on the bottom couple of steps.

They know me so well now, they've been expecting me to appear.

'No, Simmerton, but I feel as if I am suffocating. I need to be out in the air.' She opened the door fully, and her butler rose from the camp chair he'd been perching on. 'If the men have gone off after Withershaws in town, is it not most unlikely that he will be skulking around George Square?' she pleaded.

'Most, ma'am,' Simmerton agreed, and Melissa's spirits lifted. 'The colonel gave me back the keys to the basement entry. If Joanie and I accompanied you, I cannot think there would be objection to a short stroll into the Gunns' private garden.'

'My thoughts exactly. Joanie, will you help me into a coat? This shawl is likely to trip me.' The women slipped coats over their house garments and pattered down the stairs to the basement, where Simmerton held the door open a crack or two.

'It's all quiet out there, ma'am. I'll pull the doors to, but leave them unlocked.'

'Unlocked, Mr Simmerton? Zed wouldn't like that.' Joanie sounded nervous.

'Zed isn't here,' Simmerton said, and Melissa heard the seething resentment imbuing his tone. She knew it was risky to leave the doors, but as she'd said earlier, the thought of a fire was always with them, and Mrs Gunn and the servant girls were all asleep inside the house.

'We won't tell him, Joanie,' she said. 'And we will not be long away. It is simply to stretch our legs after the long evening and breathe some air.'

20

The men exchanged glances as far as they could in the gloom. Harry's brain spun with the myriad explanations there might be for such behaviour. She was being assaulted by a client or by one of her disreputable guards. Men like the oafs they'd left further back would have no hesitation in beating a girl who didn't co-operate as the visitor wished. Maybe she'd consumed too much uisge beatha or French brandy and was screaming for the sake of screaming.

'We maun gae up.' Leslie was at his side, and Zed already had the door onto the stairwell open. Harry laid a restraining hand on his elbow.

'We have no weapons beyond these sticks,' he cautioned. 'Slow and silent, if you please.' He hissed the words, but who would hear in any case as the girl screeched on?

Once into the entry, they heard pounding on a door over their heads. It was matched by a stream of Gaelic that Harry could not interpret, but anyone could hear the fear. Highland Nell was shocked and terrified.

'Sounds as if her guardians are locked out,' Harry whispered. 'That may mean Withershaws and George wanted to be uninterrupted, or . . . '

'Or the beggars have fallen out,' Zed broke into his speech. They were often thus attuned when at war, and even in peace their reactions bore uncanny similarity. It was not the moment to explore the thought, but Harry remembered how Zed felt Withershaws was surprised to learn from the countess of George's bungled attempt to abduct her. Perhaps they *had* been puppet and master, and perhaps the master had less of a grip on the strings than he believed. Perhaps Withershaws did not know how mad George was and that could be very dangerous for the English lawyer, he thought as he powered up the narrow staircase with his men at his heels.

'Stand away,' Zed ordered the dishevelled creature who was banging the panels of the door with a cudgel of sorts. When the man did not move as quickly as Zed wanted, he reached out and jerked his coat collar so that the fellow toppled and had to be caught by Percy before he fell headlong downwards.

Harry watched Zed manipulate a pick into the lock, and in an eerie moment of silence heard the tumblers. But the door still resisted.

'They've shot the bolt,' the guard moaned behind them. 'Heard it, didn't I?'

When no one answered his futile question, he sank onto his knees against a riser and then slumped round and sat. He sagged against the wall.

'How many?' Harry asked him.

'Twa. They've got ma mate in there tae. That dark yin tripped him up and then landed him a huge dunt on the back o' his heid.'

'And the girl?'

'Nell can haundle maist men,' the guard said as he rubbed his shins. 'But I doan't think they wiz interested in her wance they saw the other yin wiz there.'

'Which man arrived first?' Zed hissed the question without turning from his work at the door. He pulled and pushed the thing by its rickety handle, and Harry hoped the nails would hold while he worked up a rhythm — at least the nails of the handle. He could see Zed was trying to dislodge the ones holding the bolt or latch on the other side in place.

'The auld yin. He's been afore and he jist talked the first time. Nell wiz richt taken with him and offered him a free go when he wanted tae come again.' The man grinned and exposed a few cracked and yellowed teeth.

Harry's scalp prickled in recognition. *Highland Nell.* How far north did the girl come from, and who were her relatives? he wondered. If she spoke

Gaelic as a native, then she was not from Auchenwylde, but she might easily have family there. She might have female connections who delivered the bairns in the townships. And if she did, was it so hard to work out that one midwife might talk to another? And once they were talking, would it be unimaginable that one woman would try to trump another in their stories?

He shivered. Ghosts were dancing on his hopes of marriage to a brave girl with so much love in her heart and grace in her being.

'Your shoulder here, sir.' Zed spoke with that peremptory tone even Harry could not ignore. He moved up to the top step and together they forced the door, tumbling into a room of stinking mess and a very dead lawyer.

'His chest is lifting,' Harry said after a moment's stunned inaction. 'That's blood. Strip his coat off, Percy; help me here.'

While Harry worked to get at a wound in Withershaws's side which was staining his clothes red, he was aware of Zed and Matt Just out of his eye-line. They were cajoling George to give up the knife he was holding. Leslie made a quick inspection of the other guard and grunted. Harry was unable to work out whether he meant the man would live or was already dead, but Leslie swiftly turned him over onto his front as he had been trained, so he thought there was a chance.

The girl carried on screaming, and soon Leslie crossed to her and, lifting her around the waist, carried her out of the room and clattered down the stairs with her.

'He should be dead,' George said calmly. He allowed Zed to take the knife from him and made very little reaction when the men tied his wrists in front and shoved him onto a settle draped with women's clothing. 'He deserved to die for insulting Lady Pateley. I heard how he tried to force himself on her in Wales, and then he told me I was too far down the social scale to address her. Me! I am at least a gentleman and not a tradesman.'

Harry had forced his way through the lawyer's clothing and exposed a nasty ragged gash, but although it bled copiously, he thought it was not deep enough to have reached anything vital. Why, then, was the man unconscious?

'Did you clout Mr Withershaws?' he asked, but George refused to say anything more. Harry ran his fingers over Withershaws's scalp and found a haematoma forming towards the back. 'You did. At least that explains why he is unconscious. George you'll go to jail for this night's activity.'

'Likely be transported once the lawyers get wind of an attack on one of their own,' Zed muttered. Harry did not disagree with him. He almost lifted a prayer to the Almighty. Surely Melissa would at least be safe from him, if he were sent overseas?

Withershaws spluttered and vomited. Harry steeled his nerves, but the man stopped and tried to rise onto his knees.

'Assist me, Percy,' Harry said. Together they eased Withershaws onto his knees and then upright. They half-carried him the short distance to the revolting bed where Highland Nell plied her trade and set him down on it. Harry shuddered. How much vile illness and putrefaction was in these sheets? he wondered. There was, however, no alternative at that time, and he watched his patient carefully.

The wheezing began very soon after Withershaws came round, and Harry recognised the panic in the other man's eyes. He had seen many suffer this lack of breath, and tried to remember what action might be best. Much as he hated the lawyer, he did not wish to be responsible for his death.

'Calm, sir. You need to stay calm,' he said in a desperate attempt to help. At his side, Harry felt Percy stiffen, which made him raise his glance from Withershaws's heaving chest to find a trickle of blood escaping from his mouth. No doubt the sign Percy had reacted to, and very worrying.

Withershaws writhed on the bed. His skin was pasty and the blood began to increase in volume, carving a dark track through his day's growth of beard before it dripped onto his neck cloth. Harry stepped back. He hadn't found a wound deep enough to make the man bleed internally. There must be another. He turned to George.

'Where is the second wound, man? Quick; I need to staunch the blood.'

'Too deep for that, *Colonel* Gunn,' George said; and Harry recoiled from the malevolence in his tone and glance. He was mad beyond anything they'd feared.

Behind him, Withershaws gulped air frantically, but he could not get it down into his lungs. The struggle increased until his death agonies resounded among them. Percy moved further from the bed and left Harry alone in his attempt to ease Withershaws onto a rank-smelling bolster. It did no good. The wretched man gave out a final grunt, and then his eyes rolled back in his head. He was gone.

★ ★ ★

The company assembled in Mrs Gunn's drawing room were bleary with tiredness and gaunt with shock.

Melissa listened in horrified silence as the men recounted the story. When Harry reached the part about Withershaws's death, she had to lift her handkerchief over her mouth least she retched. The man had caused them misery in plenty, and there was little doubt that he was visiting the place in order to satisfy his baser needs, but he did not deserve to die in such a manner. No one did.

Lottie sat with Mrs Gunn, and when the older lady gave an involuntary squeal, she reached over and covered her hand with her own. Melissa knew both ladies had been very worried by the apparent disappearance of all the men except Simmerton. They were not in the house at breakfast, and the female servants had rushed around trying to do all the work left unattended as well as get the ladies up and serve breakfast. When none had appeared by eleven of the clock, Simmerton had gone to the Paxtons' house and brought back Agnes, Lottie and some tendrils of gossip about the men's experiences.

It was well into the afternoon before the bedraggled company reappeared. Uncle John was soon behind them with Kitty and Mairie. The old man sat stiff-backed, and Melissa knew he was suffering agonies of shame and embarrassment over the condition of George Gunn. But really, she thought as she watched him pass a shaky hand over his brow, what else could he have done? She got up then and crossed the room to lean over him.

'Mr Gunn, I wonder if you should go home again. I would walk with you, if you would like. Now that George is locked away and Withershaws is dead, there can be little for me to fear.' She saw his shoulders stiffen even more and hoped he did not think she blamed him in any way. On the contrary, it was his persistence that had alerted Harry and Thomas Paxton to the likelihood of such events.

'Lady Pateley is in the right, Uncle,' Harry said. 'We must all sleep now.' A yawn interrupted his words, but he recovered. 'And the legal officers have discharged us from further questions until tomorrow.'

'Will they hang George?' Lottie asked, surprising them all as she had been silent until now. Melissa looked across at her. She had aged in appearance in the last few weeks, and the edge of her assurance was worn thin. Melissa felt her husband would find a more modest woman waiting his return than the one who had waved him off.

'I think it very unlikely,' Harry said carefully. 'The man is quite mad.'

'So there is no guarantee that Melissa will be safe from his attentions?'

'I cannot believe George will ever be allowed to leave the bedlam, if that is where he is sent,' Harry said more firmly. 'The authorities will not want a man with such a dangerous obsession wandering the streets of our towns.'

'No,' Lottie agreed, although Melissa thought it was at best half-hearted. 'It does seem too great a risk for anyone in authority to allow.'

'Come, Agnes.' Thomas Paxton turned back to the room from his position at one of the windows. He had been summoned earlier by Harry and taken a coach and a cart along the high street to fetch the men. Percy, Matt, Leslie and one or two others Melissa was unable to identify had tumbled from the cart and into the basement kitchen. She knew they would have been fed porridge and rolls by Donal and cook before escaping to the attics over the soap works to sleep.

'When Donal brought the news in the early hours, I am sure you did not get back to sleep,' Thomas continued, addressing his wife, 'and I see your eyelids are dropping with tiredness. We soldiers can carry on longer, but even so, Harry and Zed are exhausted.' He walked over to his wife and eased her out of her chair by sliding his hand under her arm. 'We might return this evening, Mistress Gunn, but we will have eaten.'

Their exit marked a general departure, and within moments Melissa and Lottie were the only people left in the big room. They each smiled tentatively, but had little to say.

'I wonder where Joanie is?' Melissa asked at last. She was aware of the rather old-fashioned look her companion sent her way.

'I think we shouldn't look for Joanie in the next hour or so,' Lottie said. 'I am sure she will return to her duties when once she has attended to Zed's needs.'

'Oh,' was all Melissa managed to reply. She picked up the novel Mrs Gunn had borrowed for her from the subscription library and again tried to read it. Although it was by daylight now and not candlelight, she seemed to have little success.

★   ★   ★

'Are you making much headway with that book, ma'am?' Lottie asked eventually. 'I wondered for a moment or two whether you were holding it upside down.'

Melissa raised her eyes and waited while Lottie came fully into focus. The night had been restless. Although she didn't know about the men's adventures until late in the morning, she had been aware of wakening from time to time and wondering whether she heard them moving around.

'I did have it upside down. I was studying a stain an earlier reader has left on the paper. I'm pleased to see it because I could not have seen it two weeks ago.'

'You are improving daily, Melissa.

Your hair grows and normal colour infuses your cheeks. I am glad to see that.'

'Thank you. It is in no small way due to the care Harry and Zed have taken for me,' Melissa replied, and was glad to note Lottie responded with a tiny blush. Perhaps the older woman was coming round to the value of Harry's medical skills.

A loud clatter sounded up the stairs and they both started. Lottie was on her feet and across to the door as quickly as her long skirts allowed, but Melissa had to take more time. She knew that her recovery did not yet permit her to leap from sitting to standing without certain care.

Lottie had gone onto the landing and was leaning over the bannister rail. She straightened and turned back to Melissa.

'Excuse me, but, cook has fallen over in the basement hall. I will go down.' With that short explanation, the woman disappeared and Melissa took her place at the rail. When she had steadied herself and dared to lean out a little, a confused sight met her gaze.

Joanie was standing two or three steps up from the basement, and Lottie was beginning her descent of the final flight of stairs. But it was the mess in the downstairs hall that startled Melissa the most. It looked as if a burglar's haul had been drawn down from a cupboard and lay scattered over the flags. There were several candlesticks visible, lights flashed as if jewellery was mixed in, and a pile of rich materials slithered from cook's fingers as the woman lifted her head to respond to a remark from Lottie.

Melissa clasped her hand over her mouth. The house must have been invaded last night when she, Simmerton and Joanie walked out to the gardens. Had they disturbed a thief? She gazed around the halls and stairwell. Was he still in the house?

21

As quickly as she safely could, Melissa descended. The women were in a tizzy, and Lottie struggled to make herself heard above the conflicting shouts and accusations flying hither and yon. Eventually, she managed to sweep the whole party into the kitchen and closed the door.

'What are you making such a din over?' Lottie asked, raising her voice now to be heard. Cook looked mutinous, but subsided. The scullery girl burst into tears and dashed off to her tiny cupboard of a workspace. They heard a plate crash onto the flags, and cook raised her eyes heavenwards.

Melissa looked round for Simmerton. Spotting him at last settled into cook's big chair with a rug across his knees, she was silenced. When had the man become so old?

'I expect more sense from you, cook. The master has been up all night, and you're making enough of a row to waken the inhabitants of any kirkyard, never mind a former soldier in a state of alertness.' Lottie lambasted her mama's staff with little regard for the condition of anyone's sensibilities. Clearly, Melissa thought, it was Harry who counted here.

'Beg your pardon, ma'am, but we were frighted by the sight of the valuables. What if the thief is lurking in the house somewhere? And how did a body git in here?' Cook looked round her domain as if she might find burglars, thieves and assassins draping from her ceiling ham hooks. 'We sleep that deep, ma'am, after a decent day's work. I didna here onything.'

'Lottie, might I speak with you, please?' Melissa asked with not a little diffidence.

They left the kitchen and, picking their way carefully over the pile of valuables, climbed up to the ground floor. With Simmerton downstairs, the hall was unattended. Donal had probably gone along to the soap works dormitory to catch some sleep, too.

'I am very sorry, Lottie, but I think this invasion of your mama's house is my responsibility.' Melissa looked straight at Lottie and saw the conflicting emotions sweep her features. She took a deep breath before continuing. 'Although I promised Harry I would not go wandering in the town last night . . .'

'Wandering in the town at night!' Lottie exclaimed. 'What prompted Harry to think such a thing? No respectable woman would be wandering in the town at night.'

'He did not suspect that, Lottie. No, I did go out with Percy that time, which gave George his opportunity. However, Harry wanted to lock the house last night and take the keys away with him. I panicked a little. The fire has left me nervous about locked doors.' Melissa brought her hand to her throat and eased the lace around it. She felt her chest tighten, but knew she had to confess.

'I see,' Lottie said. 'I believe you are about to tell me you went into the gardens.'

'He will work it out in an instant and think I am not to be trusted, ever.' Melissa felt the shame of such a judgement. A tear slid unheeded down one cheek.

'Calmly, ma'am, please. You have been unwell for a long time now, and I think it is understandable that you wanted to take some air and did not want to be confined. I do not quite see how an undesirable got into the house, however.'

'We left the area door unlocked. Simmerton and Joanie came with me, and we were gone only a few moments. It looks as if that was long enough.'

'Oh dear,' Lottie said. 'Yes, and even if the person were trapped inside when Simmerton locked up again, he's had ample chance to leave amidst the chaos here this morning without anyone remarking.'

A noise on the stairs alerted them to cook's arrival from the basement. Both women turned towards her, and Melissa gasped.

'Papa,' she said.

'Is this yours, Lady Pateley, ma'am?' cook asked. 'Only, it were among the stuff downstairs. Joanie identified some of your jewellery, and it was amongst those pieces.'

'A miniature?' Lottie said quietly. Melissa drew short breaths and waited while Lottie sank onto a settle beside the front door.

She held her hand out, and cook placed the gold-rimmed miniature onto it. No doubt the thief had had an eye to the valuable frame, she thought.

I had quite forgotten I had this with me at Berwick Old Abbey. Simmerton must have tossed it into the bags when he and Percy packed that night. How much misery would we have been spared if I had only sought it out before now?

She moved slowly across to Lottie and, remembering cook's interested glances, turned back.

'Thank you, cook. Perhaps you would have some chocolate sent up for Mistress Duart and myself?' She waited while the woman dipped an infinitesimal curtsey and retreated.

'Let me see,' Lottie said abruptly, and Melissa handed the portrait to her. It was small, but she had always thought it a very good likeness of her papa.

Melissa gave the painting to Lottie and waited.

'It was not this man,' Lottie said, and burst into loud sobs. Melissa heard a door open on the floors above. Mistress Gunn could only have waited an instant before starting to come down.

'Oh, Mama,' Lottie whimpered when her mother had reached them and gathered her into her arms. 'Oh, Mama, it was not Richard Flaxxe.'

Melissa crept away and went to her own room to recover from the morning's excitements. Surely now Harry would feel released from constraint? Surely now the path was clear?

* * *

The party gathered in Mistress Gunn's dining-room in the early evening was subdued. Harry yawned occasionally, although he tried hard to conceal it by turning away or moving restlessly between the table and the windows overlooking the square. He knew Melissa was puzzled by his reluctance to address the discovery of the miniature painting, but he could do nothing to aid her. His head was full of the events of the last twenty hours or so, and making sense of it all was too difficult for him at present. Perhaps by tomorrow he would have a plan formulated, he thought.

'Harry, you are still under-slept,' his mama said as she glanced at the half-eaten food on his plate. 'Perhaps we should have kept this information from you until tomorrow.'

'It's true what you say, Mama. I find it very hard to believe that the insuperable impediments are no longer even there,' he replied quietly. Out of the corner of his eye, he saw Melissa stiffen. She had never doubted her papa's integrity for one moment, and he was proud of her for that. Did he deserve such loyalty from anyone? He was pondering over the matter when Simmerton came into the room.

'Simmerton, I fear you had a most disturbed night, too,' Harry said, and watched with interest as the old man's cheeks flared.

'I did, sir, and Mr Zed has made it abundantly clear that my behaviour fell short of what is expected in this household. I am most sorry for it, sir, and tender my resignation.'

'What?' Melissa said. Harry turned to her and was struck by the colour suffusing her cheeks. It enhanced her appearance so much and he was hard put to remember the sorry creature he'd plucked out of Berwick Old Abbey from George's attentions.

'Simmerton, you are not in Colonel Gunn's employment. It was very much my responsibility that anyone was able to come into the house. How dare Zed make such pronouncements?'

'Calmly, my dear Melissa,' Harry said, but the lady was so wound up by his lack of attention that she was not easily deflected.

'So you think to address me now, Harry Gunn, do you? Then please advise me what right your steward has to criticise my retainers.'

'None at all.'

'Exactly. What? Are you agreeing with me in order to make me desist?' She was struggling to her feet, and Donal only just managed to catch the chair before it clattered backwards onto the rugs.

'That remark is contrary, ma'am,' Harry said. It was becoming difficult to prevent a shout of laughter escaping and he furrowed his brows in an attempt to retain at least the appearance of gravitas.

Outside in the hall, voices could be heard and people moved around restlessly. Harry thought it sounded like Thomas and Agnes, and vaguely remembered Thomas's promise to return later in the day. This must be why Simmerton had come into the room, and he rose from his place.

'Mama, I cannot do justice to your dinner tonight. I am sorry. It sounds to me as if Thomas and Agnes have walked down.'

Mrs Gunn rose too, and Melissa offered the older woman her arm. It was a touching sight, and Harry turned away in case any sentiment should overtake him.

'I think you are in the right, Harry. We will go upstairs. Donal, tell cook to save what she can of the second course for tomorrow.' Mrs Gunn walked towards the door, and when Melissa released her arm to let her pass through, Harry strode over and brought her back into the room. He waited while Donal and Simmerton left, and then he clipped the door shut and turned the key.

'Now, my lady, something has been troubling me for several days. I think the moment has come when it might be put to rights.' Harry gathered his lady in his arms and kissed her soundly. And when she did not protest, he did so again.

★ ★ ★

'Harry,' Melissa said with very little heat when he allowed her to breathe. 'Oh, Harry.'

She studied his face with less anxiety than she had felt for hours, but could hardly comprehend his actions after so much silence and brooding.

'My dear, I am sorry, but the incidents last night were extremely shocking. I think this will be at the root of any intemperate remarks Zed made to Simmerton as well, and I hope we might sort out all these misunderstandings in due course.'

'You may be correct, Harry, but I was struck this morning by how much Simmerton has aged while taking care of Joanie and me since the fire. He is certainly sixty-nine or even seventy years old.' When he did not reply immediately, she glanced up into his face. She might now think *his beloved face* without any twinge of guilt. The expression she saw there stilled the breath in her lungs and sent a frisson of delightful recognition down her spine.

She felt Harry's arm slide below her knees as he lifted her and carried her across to a small sofa. 'This is very shocking, sir, when you have guests waiting your attention above.'

'Guests may wait a little,' Harry said, and his voice had a rough edge Melissa remembered from another lifetime, another love. 'What may not wait is this fire burning between us, consuming us.' His hand cradled the back of her head, and she closed her eyes as his mouth covered hers. The promise of the last weeks was there in all its intensity. Frissons of delight raced up and down her spine and moments passed in delicious, melting oblivion. All too soon, however, Harry struggled up and let her slide back to sit alone while he perched on a chair opposite.

'I wonder at you, sir, abandoning me in this shameful manner,' she teased, and the flare of light in his eyes was her reward.

'Minx,' Harry murmured, but did not return. 'I must hear your opinion on some important matters before we join my guests upstairs.'

'Such as?' Melissa wondered at the seriousness of his tone. Surely, surely, all the fog around his birth was cleared up now. 'I think now that your father must have been the distant cousin my aunt referred to in her letter. It sounds like the sort of paltry joke a man of his nature would have taken much satisfaction from.'

'Indeed, and alas, my father must

have been the Randolph Flaxxe of your aunt's letter. We may never know for sure, and as he was never heard of again, he may have gone abroad.' Harry was thoughtful until when he spoke again, and his face cleared. 'My papa took a lot of interest in shipping because he had property overseas, I suppose. One night he waved a paper around at dinner and said to my mother that he thought this was the final proof.'

'Proof?' Melissa asked in some puzzlement.

'Yes. Farquar went down with that barque from Perth in 1786. Here is a letter from Duart.'

'The present Mr Duart's papa?'

'Yes. The name meant nothing to me then, and it has only come back across the years since we started exploring my heritage. We can assume he will not reappear in years to come to tell any stories. However . . . '

Melissa stared at Harry then, because his voice was as serious as it ever became. What dreadful impediment had he thought of now?

'However, Mr David Withershaws learned of Lottie's indiscretion from someone, and I think I worked it out yesterday evening. I think he learned it from Highland Nell.'

'Who?'

'I am sorry, my dear — the girl Withershaws was visiting. She was screaming in Gaelic as we arrived, and I know that many of the country folk around Auchenwyld have relatives from the Gaelic speaking areas. I think she might be the daughter of a birthing woman.' He stopped speaking, and Melissa saw the struggle he was having to form words.

'You think her mama, or an aunt maybe, heard a story from your mama's woman,' Melissa said. She knew gossip grew and spread like mushrooms, so it was all too possible.

'Yes.'

'Harry, I cannot be happy when you are not happy. If you wish to give up the lairdship and become an ordinary gentleman with business interests in soap and medicines, I will stand by your decision.'

'That is generous of you, my dear. But you have moved in the highest circles, and many doors will be closed to us when news of my parentage leaks out. I believe it will, you know.'

'It may. But it will not close the doors we need concern ourselves with. I will give up the title when we marry,' she added. 'Truth to tell, it will be something of a relief, because I have missed my work in Papa's businesses. I wonder whether there will be a new aristocracy — or meritocracy, if you will.'

'I am glad to hear you say so, because I do not wish to go on living this lie. Much as I love Mama and respect Lottie, I cannot keep watching every shadow least it be another such as Withershaws who would make money or even sport with the knowledge.'

'Then let us go upstairs and tell them,' Melissa said, and then added,

'Tell them what?'

'It cannot make much practical difference beyond ownership of the Keep at Auchenwyld. The lawyers may need to sort it out, and if Mama is correct, it may nonetheless belong to me. The new blood in Duart's firm will advise, I'm sure.'

Melissa watched in fascination as the serious expression left Harry's face and a glint appeared in his eye. She wondered how long it might be before they joined those waiting upstairs.

We do hope that you have enjoyed
reading this large print book.

Did you know that all of our titles
are available for purchase?

We publish a wide range of high
quality large print books including:
Romances, Mysteries, Classics
General Fiction
Non Fiction and Westerns

Special interest titles available in
large print are:
The Little Oxford Dictionary
Music Book, Song Book
Hymn Book, Service Book

Also available from us courtesy of
Oxford University Press:
Young Readers' Dictionary
(large print edition)
Young Readers' Thesaurus
(large print edition)

For further information or a free
brochure, please contact us at:
Ulverscroft Large Print Books Ltd.,
The Green, Bradgate Road, Anstey,
Leicester, LE7 7FU, England.
Tel: (00 44) **0116 236 4325**
Fax: (00 44) **0116 234 0205**

THE LEGACY OF BLACKTHORN

June Davies

During a stormy winter's night, Meirian Penlan travels by stagecoach to take up a mysterious post at Blackthorn Manor. Wild and remote, Blackthorn lies amongst the great meres of Lancashire, surrounded by long-held superstitions, tales of witchcraft and uncanny occurrences. Once there, Meirian is drawn into a web of scandal, deception, blackmail and tragedy. Discovering old love letters and a terrible secret, she risks everything to set right a dreadful wrong — and unravel the disappearance of Blackthorn's medieval jewels . . .